P9-CQH-671

Dear Reader:

The book you are about to read is the latest bestseller from St. Martin's True Crime Library, the imprint *The New York Times* calls "the leader in true crime!" Each month, we offer you a fascinating account of the latest, most sensational crime that has captured the national attention. *The Milwaukee Murders* delves into the twisted world of Jeffrey Dahmer, one of the most savage serial killers of our time; *Lethal Lolita* gives you the *real* scoop on the deadly love affair between Amy Fisher and Joey Buttafuoco; *Whoever Fights Monsters* takes you inside the special FBI team that tracks serial killers; *Garden of Graves* reveals how police uncovered the bloody human harvest of mass murderer Joel Rifkin; *Unanswered Cries* is the story of a detective who tracked a killer for a year, only to discover it was someone he knew and trusted; *Bad Blood* is the story of the notorious Menendez brothers and their sensational trials; *Fallen Hero* details the riveting tragedy of O. J. Simpson and the case that stunned a nation.

St. Martin's True Crime Library gives you the stories *behind* the headlines. Our authors take you right to the scene of the crime and into the minds of the most notorious murderers to show you what really makes them tick. St. Martin's True Crime Library paperbacks are better than the most terrifying thriller, because it's all true! The next time you want a crackling good read, make sure it's got the St. Martin's True Crime Library logo on the spine—you'll be up all night!

Charles E. Spicer, Jr.
Senior Editor, St. Martin's True Crime Library

The police detectives saw the pattern repeat itself again and again. Ricardo Caputo was an incredibly skilled charmer, a modern day gigolo who latched on to women to improve his own prospects. He never wined and dined them, he let *them* do it in exchange for his company. And it was company that, at least initially, these highly accomplished women liked to keep. He gained their sympathies with stories about his poverty-stricken, abusive childhood. He gained their support with what he described as his earnest attempts at making something of himself in America. He demonstrated his flair for art, his command of five different languages. He impressed them with his athletic abilities and sexual prowess.

The frustrated investigators across the country looking at these connected and unresolved homicide cases didn't buy this charmer's tale of a tortured soul who was only looking for love. What he was, they claim, and what they believe he remains, is a cold-blooded killer whose violent temper and inability to face rejection triggered brutal, premeditated crimes.

In every sense of the word, they say, he was a *lady-killer* . . .

LADYKILLER

JULIET PAPA

ST. MARTIN'S PAPERBACKS

NOTE: If you purchased this book without a cover you should be aware that this book is stolen property. It was reported as "unsold and destroyed" to the publisher, and neither the author nor the publisher has received any payment for this "stripped book."

LADYKILLER

Copyright © 1995 by Juliet Papa.

Cover photograph by Tony Stone Images, Inc.

All rights reserved. No part of this book may be used or repro-duced in any manner whatsoever without written permission ex-cept in the case of brief quotations embodied in critical articles or reviews. For information address: St. Martin's Press, 175 Fifth Ave-nue, New York, N.Y. 10010.

ISBN: 0-312-95467-0

Printed in the United States of America

St. Martin's Paperbacks edition/February 1995

10 9 8 7 6 5 4 3 2 1

CHAPTER ONE

D r. Fernando Linares replaced the phone in its cradle and wondered what was coming. In his twenty-five years as one of the noted psychiatrists in Mendoza, Argentina, he had consulted on many important cases and had treated the predictable range of patients whose problems spanned the whole spectrum of disorders and dysfunctions.

But his caller, the lawyer Mario Luquez, was a man as prominent in his profession as Linares was in his, and he had been anxious and oddly hurried on the phone. There was someone the lawyer wanted the psychiatrist to see. "Right away," Luquez had said. "I'll send him right over. He needs an immediate evaluation."

There was a pause, and Dr. Linares heard an intake of breath on the other end. Then the words came out slowly, deliberately, as if the attorney wanted to make sure he was being understood.

"Brace yourself," he told Linares, "because you will not believe what this man is going to tell you. He's returned to Mendoza, to his mother's home, after twenty-five years. And he's admitting to a lifetime of unspeakable crimes.

"But you must believe him," the lawyer added, "because it is all true!"

Luquez said no more and had not invited any questions. Dr. Linares pushed his chair back from his desk and rubbed his forehead. It was a January day in Argentina in 1994. If the psychiatrist had chosen to open one of his office windows, the dry winds pouring off the Andes Mountains would have carried the aromas of cherry and eucalyptus and the ripening grapes from the vineyards for which the Choapa River valley in Mendoza are famous. He would have seen the blossoming light green leaves filling out the trees gracefully swaying in the soft wind.

But at that moment Dr. Linares was far from appreciating the sights and sounds of the jewel of the city that was his home. He stared blankly as he pondered the cryptic phone call, trying to sort out the questions that began swirling through his mind. He had been disturbed by Luquez's uncharacteristic behavior, his mysterious, almost curt manner. After all, he knew the attorney to be a thoughtful, considerate man, refined in the manners of his upbringing and long experienced in the exercise of professional courtesies. And Linares did not want to cross the line and disrespect his colleague by pressing for details. But, the psychiatrist thought, it was so unlike Luquez to impose and rush someone over on such short notice. And then to sum up this prospective client with such an ominous, electrifying statement!

Linares surmised that for such unusual steps to be taken, something unusual was afoot. And he shuddered at the thought of the lawyer's last remark. Despite his expertise as a cool, calm clinician seeking out clear-cut diagnoses for mental or emotional problems, he found himself wrestling with the uneasiness that began to tug at the corners of his own emotions, so he sought to shake it off by launching into a mental scan of some of his most difficult cases. But almost before he began, he knew he would conclude that there was *none* in his repertoire that came to him shrouded in such urgency and secrecy. Linares felt uncomfortable with the elusive but unmistakable sense of foreboding that began to permeate his thoughts when it came to this particular case.

The questions formulating in his mind now became clear. He accepted them as amazingly simple, yet he knew the limitlessness of the frustration of having no answers—and worse yet, fewer clues. What could this *be?* Linares wondered as he began to tap his fingers ever so lightly, but quickly and in nervous succession, on his desk. *Who* could this be? he wondered impatiently.

The psychiatrist suppressed an uncharacteristic urge to give in to his imagination; but little could his —or *anyone's*—imagination conjure up the chilling details of a life that this mystery patient was about to reveal.

It was a story too terrifyingly real, about a dizzyingly complex life in which love and murder were fatally intertwined; a twenty-five-year odyssey of violent thoughts that exploded into violent acts time and time again. Here was the master fugitive who eluded authorities as he cut a murderous swath across a continent and two countries. This was a man who in his teens was driven from his South American homeland by a war for his passions waged daily between a need to be loved and a lethal tendency to react with terrifying physical brutality when it seemed that love was about to be denied him. It was a combination of desperation and a vague notion of hope that ultimately propelled this son of Mendoza toward the United States, where he tried to escape his past and plot a blueprint for his American Dream. Instead, he followed a devastating pattern of murder, which he successfully repeated again—and again—and again—and again.

He first struck in 1971, inflicting his fatal response to what he perceived as the ultimate rejection. Twenty-year-old Natalie Brown told him she didn't want to go out with him anymore. Her body was found sprawled on the kitchen floor of her parents' spacious Long Island home. She had been stabbed eight times, the wounds suggesting that she couldn't turn away fast enough to escape the repeated slashing of the blade.

But *he* escaped the limits of the law, despite his confession to the crime and an arrest on murder charges. He avoided prosecution for the brutal killing when doctors found him mentally unfit to stand trial. His trip to an institution for the criminally insane created the opportunity for another victim to present herself.

The opportunity came in 1974, and it ended with the discovery of the bruised body of psychologist Judith Becker on the bed in her Yonkers, New York, apartment. One of her own nylon stockings had been knotted around her neck. Authorities say the twenty-six-year-old Becker had been counseling the man she knew as a killer—and dating him at the same time. Their deteriorating personal relationship triggered what was to become his trademark response. He skipped town after the murder, and his disappearance sparked a national manhunt. But that didn't deter him from his ultimate destiny to mate and murder once again.

And it didn't take long. Just a year later, in San Francisco, he moved in with film industry executive Barbara Ann Taylor. It took her only a few months to realize that she wanted him out of her life. Instead, he took hers—stomping her on the head with the metal-edged heel of his heavy work boot. The stomping, said one shocked detective familiar with the case, might have taken place over a period of ten to fifteen minutes.

He fled again, even before police knew who they were looking for, surfacing this time in Mexico City in 1977, where another live-in girlfriend was brutally slain. Twenty-five-year-old Laura Maria Gomez Saenz, the daughter of a prominent local family, was beaten to death with a pipe. The cause of death was listed as "trauma to the facial skull." Her killer forced her to drink industrial alcohol while still alive, pulled out all her teeth with pliers, and dragged her lifeless body around the wreck of her apartment. At the time of her death she was said to be two months pregnant. "Whoever did this," said the medical examiner on the case, "is a beast."

Authorities will admit to plenty of lost time when it came to tracking down this "beast." There were months and years when his whereabouts were unknown, when he never seemed to surface, when he seemed to live and travel through the shadows, the restless killer on the run. There are some segments that emerge sporadically from the curtain of mystery, all containing the familiar earmarks of violence and escape. Investigators say he raped a woman in Hawaii and ran from that crime only to return to San Francisco weeks later to kill Barbara Ann Taylor. After her murder, he hightailed it south in an attempt to illegally jump the Texas border into Mexico. It was there that federal officials nabbed him, but only on an immigration charge. Here he was—actually in custody! But within days of his arrest, this calculating killer hatched a plot and carried out a daring armed escape, knowing full well that he had to disappear before the FBI completed the background check they had already begun.

His newfound freedom once again afforded him the means and the motive for murder. New York City police detectives suspect that after killing Laura Gomez in 1977, the killer made his way back to New York City. That's where noted author and activist Jacqueline Bernard was found strangled to death. Investigators believe she had, as she often did in the past, befriended someone who needed her help and influence, someone who got to know her through the causes she supported on Manhattan's Upper West Side, someone who knew she was generous with financial assistance for the underdog. It was a tipster who gave up a name and an M.O.—a modus operandi, or method of operation—that the legion of law enforcement officials investigating this wanted murderer were by now all too familiar with.

They saw the pattern repeat itself again and again. Here was this incredibly skilled charmer, a modern day gigolo who latched on to women to improve his own prospects. He never wined and dined them, he let *them* do it in exchange for his company. And it was company that, at least initially, these highly accomplished women liked to keep. He gained their sympathies with stories about his poverty-stricken, abusive childhood. He gained their support with what he described as his earnest attempts at making something of himself in America. He demonstrated his flair for art, his command of five different languages. He impressed them with his athletic abilities and sexual prowess.

The frustrated investigators across the country looking at these connected and unresolved homicide cases didn't buy this charmer's tale of a tortured soul who was only looking for love. What he was, they claim, and what they believe he remains, is a cold-blooded killer whose violent temper and inability to face rejection triggered brutal, premeditated crimes. In every sense of the word, they say, he was a *lady-killer*.

That moniker, "Ladykiller," was also the title of a precedent-setting broadcast of the popular television show "America's Most Wanted" in July of 1991. For the first time in its history, an entire show was dedicated to profiling a single case. It was *this* case—and the response was unbelievable. The broadcast generated eight hundred calls on the night of the broadcast, and follow-up calls and alleged sightings all over the country that swelled to more than four thousand "tips" on the string of killings. The FBI estimates they pursued fifteen hundred leads in the case, leads they reluctantly admit led them only so far, but never all the way to the killer. They went so far as to distribute age-enhanced photos, but the killer negotiated his skills as a fugitive with the same inventive ease with which he picked up women by sketching them in restaurants and smothering them with compliments. He stayed on the run by remaking himself, changing hairstyle and facial hair combinations, removing tattoos, and gaining and losing weight whenever he chose. He was chameleonlike, perhaps an invisible man who was seen everywhere, but was caught nowhere.

Did the "Ladykiller" himself see the program when it aired on that hot summer night? No one can be sure, but it may have served to flush him out of a neighborhood just outside Chicago, where he had developed yet another facet of his ever-changing personality: that of husband and father of three, living in a one-family home with a front lawn and garage!

Soon after the broadcast, the house went up for sale. He pulled up stakes and disappeared once again, even keeping his wife in the dark as to his whereabouts, surfacing for the final time in Mendoza. And as in the past, the killer was on the run. But this time there was a twist. He now claimed he was saving himself—from himself.

This fugitive with four known murders under his belt would later claim that it wasn't a blood lust or the rage of rejection that fueled his urge to kill. It was the demons in his soul—demons that he feared were re-emerging in forms that he would not be able to control. He blamed "voices" for his urge to kill, and warring personalities within for his life of crime. He said he saw "broad lines" and "dots" before and during the acts of murder. He subsequently documented the self-observations of his alleged mental state, wrote them all down, and described murder after murder in a revealing "diary."

One investigator conceded that his quarry may in fact have mental problems—he had to, given the nature of his crimes—but didn't buy it as a total excuse for his butchery. "Hearing voices?" the investigator said with thinly veiled sarcasm. "He's full of shit. He's just a psychopath who's very good at lying and making people feel sorry for him. I think he's sick, but I don't think he's a schizo."

It was soon after his return to Mendoza that the world was to learn that this killer was back. But the reasons that propelled him to resurface were going to be made clear in so startling and public a fashion that not only would it take the law enforcement community by surprise, it would horrify the families of the victims, who felt the old wounds of grief and pain reopen once again. After contacting the mother he supposedly hadn't seen in a quarter of a century, the killer located his wealthy brother living in New York City. The brother hastily financed a top-flight Park Avenue attorney, who, in a matter of a few short weeks, turned the monster into a media sensation. Through a carefully orchestrated campaign designed to elicit sympathy for his client, the lawyer found eager takers in the news media. It took less than a day for the story to spread like wildfire. It headlined the *New York Times, San Francisco Chronicle,* and *Chicago Tribune*—wherever it was known that this madman had touched a life, or taken one. The effort crescendoed in an exclusive interview on the nationally broadcast ABC television news show "Prime Time Live."

But none of the multitude of stories written about

him in the weeks after his surrender answered the fundamental questions. Did he flee Argentina as a young man to find relief, or escape from perceived psychiatric problems? Or was he no more troubled than any other teenager burdened by poverty and the damage of an abusive, incomplete home?

There has been evidence to suggest that when he left for the United States in 1970, he was already an apprentice opportunist eager to perfect his craft, and that within months of settling in New York City, he'd found a way to mask his shortcomings and to shrewdly tap into the shortcomings and sympathies of others in order to quickly exploit them. In his first year in New York, he was already loaded with the coping and manipulative skills needed to confront what he already perceived as an uphill world. When he looked into the mirrors of the tawdry rooms where his poverty forced him to live, the image looking back at him was of a sweet-looking man, almost pretty, surely sensual and loaded with charm. The young man and his image were looking for a partner; more than a playmate, someone to help him gain a foothold onto his own twisted path toward an opportunity for a life better than the one he knew.

But that was a quarter century ago, and the circumstances of the present were much different. In fact, the scenario was to play itself out in a way never seen before—and the prominent Mendoza psychiatrist had no idea as to the pivotal role he virtually inherited by agreeing to meet this new client. Dr.

Fernando Linares was about to trigger a series of amazing events that would launch the nightmares of some twenty years past into the present. And except for the disturbing call from his colleague, attorney Luquez, Linares had no clue about what was to come when he answered the quiet knock on his office door.

There, stood a man as serene as the spring breeze, casually dressed in clean clothes, youthful at a distance but with receding dark hair, and showing the facial puffiness of arriving middle age; forty-four years old, short and trim, with a dimpled chin, and clearly at ease with himself. Linares gestured the man toward the *sillón,* the big easy chair where his patients usually settled in his office. He sat down as well, almost girding himself for what was to come and for which he had no frame of reference. But before he could even ask a question, it was the patient who spoke first. And when he spoke, Dr. Linares was shocked into speechlessness.

"Yo soy Ricardo Caputo. Me mandó Señor Luquez. Me quiero entregar."

I am Ricardo Caputo. Mr. Luquez sent me. I want to surrender.

CHAPTER TWO

On March 29, 1970, twenty-year-old Ricardo Caputo arrived in New York City with a valise full of clothes, little money in his pocket, and big dreams in his feverish mind. His visitor's visa, issued in Buenos Aires, was his ticket to America and to the American Dream. In the absence of cash, the currency he carried consisted of a quick wit, buckets of charm, and a winning smile wrapped around his own sad and pathetic story.

But the dream would elude him for a while, as it did for nearly every immigrant without connections who tries America's greatest and most fearsome city as a first stop. Caputo lived in a succession of seedy one-room flats, paying for his existence through a series of custodial and busboy jobs. After several months in town, he stepped up a tiny notch, working out a deal with the Barbizon Hotel on East Sixty-third Street to clean floors and do other janitorial work in exchange for a rent-free small room. It was a good arrangement for the time being, Caputo thought, but he had more ambitious plans for himself. In New York City, in midtown Manhattan, he saw the stretch limos and the eye-popping restaurant menu prices and the shiny beautiful people every day; he saw the good life, and wanted it.

Money was the answer, the key to getting anywhere, Caputo knew. He was embarrassed by the paltry sums he earned in menial jobs he disdained, but he kept a keen eye peeled for any better opportunity that came his way, however small an improvement over his current status. Sure enough, in the summer of 1970, he landed a job at the world-famous Plaza Hotel on Fifth Avenue and Fifty-ninth Street. He still wore coveralls and an apron to work, he was still a janitor, which grated against his fierce Argentinean pride: but he was a janitor at the Plaza. The pay was a little better.

Through the summer and fall, he developed a routine of cashing his paycheck each Thursday, payday, at a branch of the Marine Midland Bank on Madison Avenue at Fifty-fifth Street, five blocks from the Plaza. He had to cash his checks as soon as he got them, since his pay was barely adequate to carry him from week to week. The bank was a bustling place, right in the heart of the city's skyscrapers and office towers and on one of the great shopping avenues of the world. Men in tailored suits and expensive Italian loafers vied for sidewalk space with luxurious ladies in designer clothes and good jewelry who shuttled among Madison Avenue's expensive shops and exquisite boutiques.

Ricardo Caputo's own obvious poverty was a

source of chronic frustration, and on occasions like his bank visits, when he was forced to stand shoulder to shoulder with his well-heeled betters, it pained him like the proverbial stick in the eye.

But on one fall Thursday afternoon, the young dreamer saw a bright light in the gloom. She was one of the bank's tellers, a young and pretty woman who seemed warm and outgoing whenever she waited on him, always offering a ready and genuine smile. Her long, soft brown hair fell down past her shoulders and framed a friendly face whose eyes looked directly into his whether she was speaking or listening. She seemed . . . well, Caputo concluded, she just seemed *happy*.

Twenty-year-old Natalie Brown had every reason to be happy. It was November of 1970, and the holidays, her favorite time of year, were fast approaching. And she was going to celebrate in style because she'd made a decision: after the spring, after maybe another half year of work, she would follow in her mother's footsteps and return to school to get a nursing degree. The bank teller's job was fine, she knew, and it was exciting working in Manhattan. But it was time to knuckle down and make definite plans.

She had the luxury of time. Natalie had been raised in a cocoon of privilege and wealth, the only daughter and the youngest of the three children of Harold and Julia Brown. Harold and Julia, whom everyone called Julie, had met while he was doing his service hitch at the Fort Bragg Army Base in North Carolina. When his tour was up, the couple married and settled briefly in the Bronx as Harold began what would turn out to be a career at a Manhattan-based housewares company called Kemp and Beatley Inc. He was a salesman, soon became top salesman, and eventually skyrocketed through the ranks to become a chief executive with the successful company.

The Browns rode the wave of swift success and made the requisite move to the posh suburbs, settling in Flower Hill, a private community in Roslyn, on Long Island's tony north shore. They built a home at 68 Middleneck Road, a brick and shingle two-story structure that boasted a neatly trimmed front lawn, spacious backyard, sweeping oak trees and inviting landscaping, and enough interior room to accommodate a growing family. William was their firstborn son, followed by Edward and, on January 15, 1951, by Natalie. Right from the start, the little girl was the apple of her father's eye and the object of her mother's considerable indulgence. Julie Brown dressed her little girl in darling clothes; a blue short-sleeved dress with a scoop neck a particular favorite of mother and daughter. "They traveled together, went everywhere together," recalled Natalie's sister-in-law, Margie Lee Brown. "Her mother taught her how to swim and ride horses. She loved all her children very much, but Natalie was a very special girl."

Natalie's bedroom was a symphony in pink and white. The coverlet on her queen-sized bed matched her curtains, flecked in black and gray. The child growing into a young girl and then into a teenager always treasured her white vanity, where she'd spend hours combing her long hair and experimenting with makeup. She graduated Roslyn High School in 1969, and in her yearbook, *The Beacon*, the entry described her as a fun-loving teenager whose first loves were swimming and horseback riding.

Natalie never saw the bank job as the beginning of a career; it was just a temporary stop on the way to who knows what—but at least something better. But she did the job well, because she did everything well and took pleasure in her own competence. Because of that, she always had a stream of steady customers, even if there were shorter lines facing other tellers.

It was a busy afternoon when she looked up to notice the young man standing on her line; he had a dimpled chin and regarded her with a shy smile. She knew he was a regular and always stood on her line no matter how long it was. He'd done it for several weeks now, and she had a vague memory of his being pleasant, not much beyond that. And, oh yes, she thought: his paychecks weren't very impressive. Still, she was mildly curious, especially since she felt his eyes never leaving her window. She answered his smile with one of hers as he finally stepped up for his turn and slipped his folded paycheck across the counter between them.

She was surprised when she unfolded the check

and another piece of paper fell onto the counter. It was a note, written in a fine hand.

"I'd like to meet you," the note said.

She was startled by the note's contents, yet flattered by the bold maneuver; she was only twenty, after all, and not all that experienced in the ways of men. As she looked up from the note, her lips gave way to a warm smile and she looked closely at the author. She noticed his lean physique and his stylishly unkempt soft brown hair. The smile in his intelligent eyes turned quickly into a gentle gaze of longing. Unthreatening, sweet, so *personal*. Why not? she thought. They agreed to meet when she got off work.

For Ricardo Caputo, the gambit had paid off. He'd been thinking about the pretty bank teller for weeks and finally had decided to make his move. As he walked the city, waiting for her shift to end, he couldn't believe his good fortune. New York City suddenly seemed like the friendliest, most promising city in the world.

Their relationship began quickly and intensified as the months went by, fueled by both the young couple's similarities and differences. Her adventurous spirit and love of the outdoors were a good match for his skills at swimming, camping, and hiking. She was intrigued by his foreign roots and soft-spoken lilting speech. He was an exotic, far outside and beyond her suburban Long Island existence. And that very existence, that leafy oasis of Long Island gentility, was exactly what he'd always wanted without ever having known in detail what form it would take. They saw each other more frequently.

During the week, Natalie visited Ricardo in his meager room at the Barbizon Hotel, but he much preferred spending time at her graceful Long Island home. He ingratiated himself with her family and soon became a regular weekend guest. Natalie's parents even set up a room in the basement just for him, telling her how impressed they were by his artistic and athletic abilities, as well as his command of several languages. Around Natalie's family he was pleasant, dependably amiable, and full of fun, constantly challenging her brothers to games of checkers, which he won or lost with equal good cheer, never wanting to look too clever or too good, which would upset the delicate but positive framework he'd carefully carved for himself within this family.

"He was a nice, polite, charming South American boy," Ed Brown would recall later.

Charming, yes; but scheming too. As soon as Natalie's parents embarked on an extended European vacation, in April of 1971, the amiable South American boy moved in full-time, giving up his room at the Barbizon. When Harold and Julie Brown returned, the arrangement abruptly ended, Ricardo moving back to the city reluctantly and taking a room at the Park Savoy Hotel on West Fifty-eighth Street.

But any fears of permanent damage were allayed in Caputo's mind when his new "family" continued to welcome him into the fold. In fact the Browns still trusted Caputo so thoroughly, they raised no objections when he and Natalie embarked on a series of travels. There was a quick trip to the Virgin Islands, then a languid hitchhiking tour cross-country to San Francisco and back. In the summer, Ricardo and Natalie backpacked through Europe, and talked about marriage.

But the European trip was a benchmark in more ways than one in the young couple's relationship. As Caputo kept talking about marriage, Natalie Brown subtly began pulling away. There was trouble between them, beneath the surface, at first; the two were heading down divergent paths as Natalie began to think about pursuing other avenues in her life. Caputo had no inkling as yet. In fact, he was growing more sure that he had grabbed onto the golden ring. He talked about bringing Natalie back with him to Argentina.

The Brown family would later claim there never was a formal engagement; certainly, the busboy/ janitor never gave his intended a ring. Natalie's family said they knew her real plans, plans she never revealed to Ricardo and certainly did not include him. She wanted to move on with her life, they would recall; she was going to return to school, get her nursing degree. Ricardo Caputo was a boyfriend, not a fiancé, as far as they knew.

July 31 of that summer was a Saturday night. Ricardo and Natalie, back from Europe, were going to spend the weekend at the Brown home. Natalie's brother William arrived at the house late in the afternoon with his date, and her other brother Ed was preparing to work a night shift as a dispatcher with the Salerno Cab Company nearby. Julie Brown cooked an early dinner for her children and their friends, as she and Harold were due to attend a friend's anniversary party in Queens.

When the parents left and dinner was over, William and his date left for their own night out, and Ed, Ricardo, and Natalie repaired to the rear den to watch television. They all decided to watch the Marx Brothers in *A Night at the Opera*.

Ed remembers, "Ricardo was laughing in all the right places, he was into it. They were going to spend the night at the house. I didn't notice anything that seemed wrong. They weren't arguing . . . they were just watching the movie, and laughing." Ed left for his job before the movie ended.

But all was not well between Natalie and Ricardo. Earlier in the day the two had argued, and Ricardo had the uneasy feeling that she was pulling away— out of his reach—and determined to stay that way for good.

Now, with Ed gone, the two were alone. According to Ricardo's later statement, he'd been uneasy all day, anxious about where he stood with Natalie. Once they were alone in the house, he said, he sought reassurance. He brought her to her bedroom, the pink and white hideaway where they'd been lovers so many times. But this time she broke away from his clinch, refusing to make love. She got off the bed and got dressed.

He followed her downstairs, to the kitchen, becoming more distressed by the minute. He made another advance, pressing himself upon her, but she pulled away again, rejecting him. He was confused, hurt, and the wellsprings of his anger began to break the surface; he couldn't believe she was pushing him away. And he refused to believe what she was saying. Her interests were somewhere else, she told him. Perhaps even with *someone* else. They began shouting at each other. The situation as he recalled it later was absolutely overheated. Then, he said, she called him . . . a "spic."

His rage at her rejection spun the caldron of his emotions beyond the boiling point. He was being treated *as if he didn't matter,* as if their whole relationship didn't matter. In those white-hot seconds, Ricardo Caputo could not believe, could not face the fact, that there was no chance he was ever going to be a part of her life—the good life that he'd gotten used to and wanted more of and believed he deserved. And then, *finally,* to be called a *spic!* The word flashed unwanted pictures through his mind, his boyhood poverty, the cheap hotel rooms, the dirty dishes and filthy bathroom floors.

He was standing by the utility drawer in the kitchen, that word still coursing through him. There was a carving knife there and he grabbed for it, lunging in a single murderous motion at the pretty young woman who stood before him. She tried to turn away from him but he kept swinging the blade, twice into her chest, twice into her back when she spun beneath the initial blows, then once in the ribs and three times into her stomach as she fell to the floor, on her back, the life seeping out of her.

Breathing hard, still holding the knife, he saw that her blood had sprayed all over his shirt. He dropped the knife, tore off the shirt, and left the Brown family home by the front door. He discarded his bloodied shirt in a trash can by the curb, and ran into the summer night, a killer for the first time.

CHAPTER THREE

It was about eight-thirty P.M. and Officer Pete Cucchiera was enjoying a quiet night tour at the Nassau County Police Department's Sixth Precinct when the phone rang. Cucchiera listened to the frightened, almost hysterical voice of a young man on the other end of the line. Someone with an Hispanic accent, the cop noted, though the caller's words were chillingly clear.

"I just killed someone. Please come get me!"

Cucchiera asked a few quick questions, told the caller to stay put, and dispatched officers Larry Myron and Teddy Mierceziewski to an Esso station on Northern Boulevard off Mineola Avenue in Roslyn. The two officers drove hard, top lights and siren splitting the moderate traffic that often made Northern Boulevard move below the speed limit.

When they got to the service station, Ricardo Caputo was sitting on the curb in front of the public telephone he'd used to call police. He rose to greet the two officers, but his first words were incoherent, and his bloodstained hands kneaded his own torso as the cops moved in on him. Then he blurted out, "I need help. I just killed Natalie."

They escorted Caputo to their cruiser and, once he was secured in the backseat, they tried to get him to tell the basics. He flipflopped between several narratives, perhaps afraid to admit the worst. First, he said "someone" was hurt, then it was his girlfriend. Eventually he admitted the truth—that he'd killed his girlfriend, and that she was in her kitchen, dead.

To check their prisoner's veracity, the cops asked him to write the location of the crime in their notepad, which he did without hesitation. They radioed for additional manpower and drove the quick half mile to the address Caputo had written down: 68 Middleneck Road in Flower Hill. It was dusk, daylight was fading fast; but police felt if they got there quickly enough, they'd have enough light at the crime scene to keep them from missing something, some critical piece of evidence outside the house that might be obscured by nightfall and then trampled accidentally by the crowd of people certain to be arriving over the next several hours.

When they pulled up outside the house, the front porch light was on, just as Caputo claimed. By that time, additional blue and orange Nassau County police cars converged on the scene, followed quickly by an arriving ambulance. The flashing lights lit up the oncoming night and triggered the typical commotion that attends any crime scene. Outside lights were being turned on in most of the homes surrounding number 68, neighbors emerging tentatively as they made the unavoidable connection between the flashing lights of a half-dozen police and emergency vehicles and the near certainty that something awful had happened to one of their very own.

One neighbor spotted a car from the Salerno Cab Company cruising slowly past the scene and flagged the driver down, knowing that one of the sons of Harry and Julie Brown worked for the company. "Tell Ed to get home," the neighbor instructed the driver. "Something is terribly wrong . . ."

By that time the police had entered the home. They found Natalie Brown's body sprawled faceup on the kitchen floor, clad in jeans and a silver-colored shirt. "There didn't appear to be a real big struggle," recalled Detective William Coningsby. "There was blood, of course, but not a massive amount of it. It appeared to have happened just the way Caputo said it did." Coningsby left the murder scene and quickly inspected the rest of the house, which he found to be "immaculate." In Caputo's basement "room" he found a few articles of the suspect's clothing and his traveling bag.

Once Caputo was handed over to the detectives from the Homicide Squad, who'd arrived and taken charge, the rest of the job of securing the crime scene, recording its details, and collecting the evidence continued. Photos were taken and fingerprints lifted, the floors and other surfaces combed and patted for possible hair and skin fragments. It was routine, deliberate work, conducted mostly in silence by men who'd done it before.

At ten o'clock, more than two hours after Caputo had led the first police cruisers to the Brown home, Frank Dillon, the new chief of the county's Homicide Bureau, pulled up in his own car.

He took a beat, surveying the scene from the street. Neighbors were standing in clusters, batting around the rumors that were already making the rounds.

"It's awful," said Shirley Lester, one of the neighbors. "I heard poor Natalie was hacked to death. They said her boyfriend did it. They said he just lost his job and he was afraid he was losing her too . . ."

Dillon shook his head, marveling at the swiftness of the grapevine and at both its accuracies and inaccuracies. He strode toward the house, the adrenaline of the excitement of another big case overriding his genuine weariness.

He'd only been bureau chief for a few weeks, and he'd been swamped from the start by his first case in the new position. A New York City cop who lived with his wife and kids on the south shore of Long Island had apparently cracked under the pressures of both his job and his studies for the sergeant's exam. There'd been money troubles in the household too, and when his wife returned home one day and joked that she'd just spent all the retroactive pay due him because of his police union's just-completed contract renegotiation, he hadn't seen the humor. Instead he grabbed his service revolver and ran after her, and when she locked herself in the bathroom, he pumped six shots through the door. She was found dead on the tiled floor. It was a helluva first case for the new boss to catch, and Dillon's task was complicated by the additional pressures brought to bear whenever a New York City cop was involved in a homicide—either as victim or killer. But the initial work was done and the case began moving through the system.

And now, Dillon thought, here we go again.

The victim on the kitchen floor of 68 Middleneck Road was another young female, but Dillon's first thought was that the scene looked considerably less grisly than his first view of the cop's dead wife in the bathroom. But dead is dead and murder is murder, he thought reflexively, thinking too that he still faced the uncomfortable but inevitable job of telling the loved ones what had happened while regarding them also as important witnesses. Ed Brown had shown up and was apparently in control of himself, explaining where his brother and his parents were and when everybody was expected back. Dillon waited patiently and was standing at the front door when Harry and Julie Brown returned home. Of course, they were overwrought at his description of what had happened, but Harry, he thought, seemed to understand why the police would not allow him inside.

Not so Julie Brown.

"I explained to them both," Dillon recalls, "that their daughter was lying dead on the kitchen floor and could not be moved until the medical examiner looked at her. The mother, Julie, was quite anxious to come in anyway, and it took quite a bit of doing to keep her out of the kitchen. She couldn't understand what had happened. Her daughter was in there, that's what she knew, and she wanted to go to her daughter."

It was understandable in the moment, but friends and relatives of Julie Brown say she never did seem to fully understand or accept her precious child's horrible end. For years she would keep Natalie's room just as it was, in pink and white, and would leave some of her daughter's favorite robes and dresses in the closet. Natalie's books stayed where they'd been. Sometimes in the afternoons, a relative said, for years after the murder, Julie Brown would go up to her daughter's room and take a nap in her daughter's bed.

On the night of the murder, though, Dillon waited until Julie Brown had settled into the benumbed shock that he'd seen at similar scenes in the past. Family members clung to each other, detectives hovering nearby to offer support or ask questions as appropriate. The medical examiner arrived, did his work, and left. The body was removed. Frank Dillon returned to Sixth Precinct headquarters to take his turn with the killer.

He would have to wait, though. Detective Bill Coningsby was still working on the prisoner in an interrogation room, pressing and cajoling for details. Coningsby's years of experience taught him to be long on patience because in the end he had time on his side. After several hours Coningsby had come up with the goods; Ricardo Caputo was still narrating what would turn out to be a six-page signed confession.

"He said basically that he was in love with Natalie," Coningsby recalled, "but that she'd started saying things that morning that suggested she'd found another guy. His answer to her, in effect, was 'You're leaving me, I'm not part of your life anymore—what are you doing?' "

Family members would later tell police that Natalie did not in fact have another boyfriend, guessing that she'd said she did because she thought it would get her out of the relationship with Caputo.

Coningsby summed it up this way:

"She first explained to him that she was going back to school and that it was best that they each get on with their lives. Then it was the other boyfriend, and that didn't work, and finally she made some derogatory remark about him being Spanish. She seemed to be saying, 'You're a friend, we walked around Europe together, we had a good time and lots of good memories, but good-bye Charlie, I'll see you . . .' " Coningsby added, "He was not an easy guy to say good-bye to."

When Dillon got his turn, he was startled by how angry Caputo was because he thought Natalie had been teasing him. "But what struck me first," he said, "was that the more Caputo spoke, the lower his voice got. It got lower and lower, to the point where I could hardly hear him. It was as if he was retreating from us, retreating from the world."

But neither Dillon nor his detectives had any doubts that Caputo was in full control of his faculties. Coningsby said, "He spoke fluently to me, distinctly. There were no signs of hearing voices or anything of that nature." Matt Bonora, commanding officer of the Homicide Squad, added, "He was clear and concise and right on the button. About everything. He was a rejected lover, that's what he was. He never indicated he was having any other problems, nothing about hearing voices. In fact I think it was when he was in jail for a while and had gotten a bit of a jail-house education—that's when he was hearing voices and all kinds of things."

Caputo spent his first night in jail and was arraigned the next morning on the murder charge. The grand jury action on Indictment #32240 was swift:

The Grand Jury of the County of Nassau, by this indictment, accuses the defendant of the crime of murder, committed as follows: The defendant, Richard S. Caputo, on or about the 31st day of July, 1971, in the County of Nassau, State of New York, with intent to cause the death of Natalie M. Brown, did cause the death of said Natalie M. Brown by stabbing her with a knife.
    Dated: August 5, 1971
    William Cahn, District Attorney

* * *

Caputo continued to be held at the Nassau County Jail after his indictment, but it wasn't long before word filtered back to the case detectives that something was up regarding their notorious subject.

"First thing we heard," Coningsby recalled, "was that Caputo was talking to the deceased. Talking to Natalie. I told the D.A., I had to because it was the law."

The result was that the usual pretrial hearings were delayed and replaced by competency hearings. Caputo was examined several times while the process of moving toward a criminal trial was delayed. By October, court-appointed psychiatrists concluded he could not understand the charges against him or aid in his defense, and the case judge issued his ruling: Ricardo Caputo was mentally incompetent to stand trial for the murder of Natalie Brown.

Frank Dillon recalls: "It seemed to be pretty unanimous that he was not in good shape at the time mentally. That doesn't mean he was insane at the time of the killing, only that he was not competent to stand trial, not able to understand issues. There wasn't any big argument about it."

Within two weeks of the ruling, Caputo was committed to the State Department of Mental Hygiene, and on November 15, 1971, he was transferred out of prison and shipped up to the maximum security Matteawan State Hospital for the Criminally Insane.

The law said there were to be periodic case reviews

and evaluations, and there were, and for more than two years the judges presiding over Caputo's case simply continued to sign Orders of Retention.

Under normal circumstances Caputo would in effect have been serving a life term, albeit in a hospital rather than a prison. Matteawan gave the appearance of being a grim, impregnable fortress, a complex of dull red brick structures surrounded by fences topped with razor wire. It sat on a hill, and in the winter months was almost always shrouded by a thick blanket of snow.

Ricardo Caputo hated it. Whether his jailhouse "conversations" with Natalie Brown, back in Nassau County, had been real or imagined, they'd led to a sentence of lifetime incarceration in this awful place where the food was horrible, his resources limited, his hospital mates a collection of misfits and psychopaths. And whether Caputo himself was "mentally incompetent" or not, his own mind had cleared sufficiently at Matteawan for him to see his terrible dilemma: he was being kept from getting on with his life.

It was a classic Catch-22, Caputo knew. If he was crazy, he would stay at Matteawan forever. If his mental state "improved," he would have to go back to court, where the prosecutors would be waiting with his signed confession and all the evidence, and he would face the prospect of spending the rest of his days in jail.

But in the fall of 1974 a window of golden oppor-

tunity opened in front of him. A new psychologist
had been assigned to his case. As Ricardo Caputo settled on a bench seat at one of the long tables in the
room set aside for doctor-patient consultations, he
was startled to notice that his new shrink was a
woman. A young woman, a pretty brunette. Her eyes
were kind, and looked directly at him as she extended her hand to greet him and introduce herself.
They were alone in the room.

"Hello, Ricardo. My name is Dr. Judith Becker."

CHAPTER FOUR

It was the autumn of 1973. The year was turning the corner, but for Judith Becker it held the promise of new beginnings. At age twenty-six she'd completed a postgraduate internship and was now embarking on her career, having been accepted for a full-time position in her field. In late September she was starting out as a staff psychologist at Matteawan State Hospital, a maximum security facility for the criminally insane located in upstate New York.

It was the job of her dreams, just what she wanted. In her years of study she'd become especially intrigued by the motivations and forces behind criminal behavior and the routes toward rehabilitation. She'd graduated in 1970 with a degree in psychology from Central Connecticut State College, and two years later obtained her master's at St. John's University in Queens, New York. Her internship had been spent at what was then called Grasslands Hospital, in Westchester County (it's now called the Westchester County Medical Center), and though her work there was primarily with children, work she found delightful, the job at Matteawan was the one she wanted.

Along with her new position, Judy had also moved into a new apartment, moving from Queens to 495 Odell Avenue in Yonkers, a city twenty miles north of New York City, in Westchester County. The building was a modern, though modest, high rise with double glass safety doors and a rear-lot parking space for her new 1972 metallic-bronze Plymouth Duster. She'd chosen a cozy three-room apartment on the third floor. For Judy Becker, the apartment was the first real home she'd set up as an adult away from her parents, but she remained close to her family, which included her older sister Jane. So it helped that her apartment was right near the Saw Mill River Parkway, a major north-south route that was convenient to both her job and her parents' home in Connecticut.

Henry and Jane Becker had moved from Long Island to Connecticut when Judy was eight years old, settling in the old city of Bridgewater. Located twenty-five miles north of Danbury, Bridgewater is a former farming community turned into a living picture postcard of old-fashioned New England charm. Some of the Becker's neighbors were wealthy weekenders, while others were year-rounders who commuted by rail to upscale jobs in New York City and returned at night to their own little corner of the good life. The Beckers weren't merely residents of their community, they were active participants as well. Henry Becker served as first selectman—the equivalent of mayor—for twelve years, while Jane

Becker worked as a secretary in the Burnham School, the local grammar school that both her daughters attended. The Beckers provided a comfortable and loving life for their daughters, encouraging them in their studies and making certain they knew that even after they graduated they were always welcome at home.

Judy especially visited often, spending many weekends with her parents. But she'd also come to enjoy her independence, and part of the reason she chose Yonkers rather than a community even closer to her new job was because it was a quick hop to New York City. Judy liked the city's hustle and bustle and often went to town to shop and browse the bookstores on Saturday afternoons. She was an avid reader and moviegoer—in fact, she so enjoyed the movie *The Sting* with Robert Redford and Paul Newman that she saw it twice taking her mother with her the second time.

A new job, a new car, a loving family, and the most exciting city in the world just down the road—it was a happy time in Judy Becker's life. She was unfazed by what some might have thought to be the intimidating job of working with mentally ill criminals, though she was struck by the forbidding setting of Matteawan State Hospital. It seemed such a gloomy place, the dull red brick buildings ringed by security fencing. The hospital was located directly across the Hudson River from the United States Military Academy at West Point. The young cadets, with their bright scrubbed faces and crisp uniforms, were worlds away from the troubled patients warehoused on the opposite shore.

Typically, Judy dove into her new job with a vengeance, immersing herself in the case files for each of her patients. Her conscientiousness and dedication were no surprise to those who knew her. "She was a happy person," her mother Jane said, "and she absolutely loved her job. She was totally committed to psychology."

Judy thrived on the toughest cases, working on the ward where the most difficult patients were housed. They were the men who were accused of violent or deadly acts and who had been declared "dangerous and incapacitated" by the courts. Her parents, hearing her stories about her work during her weekend visits, marveled at her lack of fear. "Judy told all of the men on her ward that if they needed a friend, she would be their friend," her mother said. "Judy was always a terrific friend, from the time she was a kid, and friendship was what she thought those men needed."

If one man on the ward needed a friend, it was Ricardo Caputo. He'd been a patient at Matteawan for more than two years, ever since he'd been declared incompetent to stand trial for the murder of Natalie Brown. He hated the setting at Matteawan, but now, with a new psychologist on the scene, he was curious to see whether she was going to do anything to improve his plight.

Their first meeting had been brief and clinical, but productive in that they seemed to hit it off well, communicating and relating in a pleasant and positive way. Over the next few weeks Judy Becker became more involved in Caputo's treatment, increasing her consultations and the time spent in each session. Her patient appeared to be responding remarkably well and seemed genuinely interested in working with her.

For his part, Caputo realized early on that hers was a sympathetic ear. He could be open with her, more open than he'd chosen to be with any other psychologist, and he quickly and graphically revealed his innermost torments about his abusive childhood and the simmering resentments he held for his mother and stepfather. He'd told the story before, but never to such a thoughtful, sympathetic audience. Their consultations were turning into personal conversations, as she responded to his need to be understood and he fed into her genuine desire to help. Soon they were calling each other by their first names—he anglicized his and said he preferred "Richie." For her, Judy was fine. The less formal their sessions became, the more they progressed in their interpersonal discovery. She was good and wholesome and genuinely interested in him and in his story. He twirled his skills and talents for her, delighting her, charming her, and she became more and more responsive.

There arrived the day, inevitably, when the line was crossed. During one of their "sessions," Caputo was impressing her with a series of sketches he had drawn. He held back one to show her last. She delighted in his work, and now, he quietly pushed the last piece of paper across the table.

"I made this for you," he told her. He had sketched a stunning likeness of her, from memory, he said, and now was offering it as a gift.

"Oh, Richie," she said, "it's beautiful."

The boundaries of the doctor-patient relationship had now blurred completely. Caputo felt as "normal" as he'd ever felt, the instrument of his healing an attractive woman who believed him and touched him in many ways. But he was making progress on another front in that he was paving the way for a masterful manipulation and eventual control of his destiny in—or possibly out of—this awful place. For Judy, the reality of what had developed was both strange and confusing—strange, because she seemed to be helping a troubled and formerly violent patient toward such remarkable progress, and in such a short time; and confusing, because she could not deny that she was getting personally involved with that patient.

They had known each other only a month when, on October 17, Ricardo Caputo was transferred out of Matteawan and placed in a less secure facility, the Manhattan Psychiatric Center on Wards Island, which sits in the middle of the East River beneath the Triborough Bridge. No one has ever fully explained the controversial move, which violated a standing order of the court. Authorities speculated that Dr. Judith Becker played some role in the transfer so her "patient" could be closer to her, and, because of the furlough privileges at Manhattan Psychiatric, he would actually be allowed as an "improved patient" to leave the grounds and visit her. Dr. Becker did not have the authority to unilaterally effect the transfer, but she did have influence because of the evaluations she submitted.

Dr. John Wright, then Assistant State Commissioner for Mental Health, provided a partial explanation. He said court decisions at the time were prompting monumental changes in the treatment and incarceration of mentally ill patients, resulting specifically in decisions to move those patients not convicted of crimes out of prisons and into less secure mental hospitals. Caputo, of course, had never been convicted because he'd never stood trial for the murder of Natalie Brown. Dr. Wright explained, "Caputo was a model patient. He was not hostile or sick. It was felt after review that he could be treated in a nonmaximum facility. We no longer considered him dangerous, but he had not recovered his competency to stand trial . . ."

Neither that explanation or any other satisfied Harold Brown, whose daughter Natalie had been stabbed to death two years ago by the patient who was no longer considered dangerous. Brown had been keeping tabs on Caputo's incarceration, and after he learned of the transfer, called Nassau County Prosecutor Frank Dillon in a near-rage. "He was really upset," Dillon recalled. "He thought Caputo was being treated like a royal guest rather than as an inmate and confessed murderer. He felt Caputo should be worked on psychologically to get him in shape to stand trial. He wanted Caputo tried . . ."

For Caputo, with no trial to worry about, it was a win-win situation. He now enjoyed more freedom than at any time since his arrest, and he believed he'd won that freedom because he'd won over his psychologist. This would be different from Natalie Brown, he assured himself. Judy Becker was not only someone he desired, someone who had willingly entered into a relationship with him, but was also someone who might be healing him. This relationship would not come crashing down, as had happened with Natalie; there would be no rejection in the end, he thought. He pursued her boldly, confidently, his situation getting better by the day. As an "improved patient" at Manhattan Psychiatric, he enjoyed grounds privileges and even weekend passes to travel off the island, unmonitored.

He began spending his weekends at Judy's apartment in Yonkers.

And Judy Becker began a new phase in her own life—living a lie.

* * *

Caputo settled in quickly and comfortably on Wards Island, learning the ropes and ingratiating himself with the staff. He worked four hours a day in the community store, making sandwiches and cheerfully waiting on customers. He involved himself in vocational programs and met often with a rehabilitation counselor. He told the new staff psychologist assigned to his case that his mental state was rapidly improving during his stay on the island.

But if his mental state was improving, his behavior in other ways was not. He started leaving the premises whenever he pleased, without the benefit of furloughs, and would show up unannounced at Judy's door. Neighbors at the Odell Avenue apartment building said the couple was obviously dating and said they often saw Caputo there. Judy told some of her friends about "Richie," but it's not known how much she told them or how much of what she told them was the truth. Dating a patient? And a patient who was a confessed killer? It was not a "truth" she could easily reconcile in her increasingly troubled mind. Perhaps it was no coincidence that as their relationship continued, she signed up for a course entitled "Ethics and Human Nature" at a nearby community college. The course did not help her resolve her problem. She was still seeing "Richie."

Inevitably, Judy's parents learned about her new "friend." On a hot Saturday morning in July of 1974,

Judy called her mother before driving up for a planned weekend in Connecticut.

"My friend Richie is here," she told her mother, "and I was wondering if I could bring him up?"

Her mother told her it would be fine. Judy told her Richie was a colleague from the Manhattan Psychiatric Center on Wards Island, and that they'd met each other in the course of their work.

It was the Big Lie that would be told again and again.

The drive north in Judy's Duster was a pleasant hour's ride away from grubby Wards Island and into the fresh country air. Caputo looked out happily as they cruised through neighborhoods of spacious homes and glorious greenery. The Becker home was filled with relatives and friends, who greeted Judy warmly and welcomed her "colleague" to Connecticut.

Judy's mother said of Richie, "He wasn't here very long. He talked a lot, I remember that. He evidently knew several languages and he talked about learning karate."

Judy's older sister Jane stopped by for about an hour and recalled her impressions of Richie.

"A nice-looking young man," Jane said. "Very pleasant, talkative and outgoing. He was very charming. He had an accent but he spoke English very well. We were told at the time that he was from Argentina, that he had a family back there and that he was involved in some family business. There was nothing in his appearance or manner, nothing at all, that would have made you think twice or be at all suspicious of him . . ."

Ricardo Caputo was having a day to remember, perhaps the signal day in his relationship with Judy Becker. He was clearly relaxed and enjoying himself, Judy's family and friends were treating him like he belonged. He lounged on the lawn furniture and cooled himself in the Beckers' in-ground pool. Here was the lap of luxury, and he was sitting right in it. He liked the fit. He was determined: this time it won't get away from me.

But Judy, troubled by her deception of the people she was closest to in the world, was riven by second thoughts. She decided to keep things at a distance by cutting Richie's visit short, offering him a ride to the train station so that he could return to Manhattan Psychiatric and she could spend the rest of the weekend with her parents.

Caputo was sullen and confused on the drive to the Brewster station. Only an hour ago he was convinced he'd arrived at the life he'd always sought. Now the woman who was the ticket to that life was sending him away.

In the next few weeks Judy made it plain that she wanted to send Ricardo Caputo out of her life. She told him she planned on spending all her weekends with her family in Connecticut, so that his weekend visits to Yonkers would have to end. Neighbors said they heard frequent loud arguments from Judy's apartment when Caputo was there. Caputo's rage was building; a friend later said he told her, "I'll show you, I don't have to come here. I won't come for two months." But when she didn't protest too much, he became even more bitter.

Here was the same pattern, repeating itself. When he finally believed he was thoroughly entrenched in the relationship that would provide for all his needs, the object of his affections was heading for the exit. He just couldn't understand or accept the rejection and struggled to find a way to hold on to some chance of salvaging the situation.

Judy was conflicted. She knew she had to end the relationship—in fact she later confided to a friend, "I feel like I have a monkey off my back"—but in the last weeks she'd come to see Caputo as a patient once again. A patient who was dissembling. Perhaps their arguments and his inability to accept what she was saying had caused her to fear him for the first time. When he stopped by her apartment in the second week of October and said he wanted to make amends, she did not send him away.

"I'm really sorry I've been so angry," he said. "Hey, I have some friends who want to take a boat ride next weekend, and we're invited. Would you like to come?"

Judy agreed and later that week told her parents of her plans. She said she'd call them when she got back from the boat ride Sunday night.

* * *

Judy Becker never called. And because she always called when she said she would, her parents grew increasingly concerned as dusk turned to night on October 20, 1974. They called her apartment time and again, finally retiring uneasily for the night. Jane Becker especially was convinced that night that something was terribly wrong, and that feeling was only intensified by a phone call early the next morning from Judy's supervisor at Matteawan State Hospital. Judy had not shown up for work, and hadn't called in either. That had never happened before.

Herbert Kaplan, the chief psychologist at Matteawan, later told reporters, "We didn't even know she wasn't here until her supervisor called her extension to compliment her on some very good therapeutic work she'd been doing with her patients. And there was no answer."

The Beckers could sit still no longer. They called their daughter Jane, who rushed home from the school where she worked as a special education teacher, and asked her to man the phone while they drove to Yonkers. It was only an hour's drive to Judy's apartment, but that morning it seemed like an eternity.

It became a journey toward their worst nightmare. Even more horrific was Mrs. Becker's startling premonition, one only a mother could know. One that repeated itself all morning and kept forcing its way into her mind on that interminable ride to Yonkers.

"I just knew she was dead," Jane Becker recalled. "These are things that occur to you as a mother. I even told my brother, I said, 'Judy is dead,' before I even knew she was dead.

"And I knew it was him."

CHAPTER FIVE

Henry and Jane Becker arrived at their daughter's apartment building around noon. They found the superintendent, who accompanied them to the third floor, but no key was needed. The door was unlocked.

It was a shocking scene. Judy Becker's lifeless body was sprawled across her bed, clad only in nylon panties. Her face and head had been pummeled by repeated blows. Police said it could have been an iron bar, a baseball bat, or simply fists propelled by astonishing force. And around her neck, a pair of Judy Becker's stockings—knotted and pulled tight.

The first Yonkers Police Department units arrived within minutes of the superintendent's phone call. The scene was quickly cordoned off as the detectives got to work. They dusted for fingerprints, looked for missing property or for evidence of a robbery, took scores of photographs and began interviewing neighbors. One third-floor resident said she heard arguing, then screaming, and then silence at about five P.M. the day before. For some reason she never called the police. Others in the building said they'd seen a man fitting Ricardo Caputo's description at the apartment building the day before, early in the day. It seemed a boat ride was never in the cards. Police also determined in short order that Judy's wallet and her Plymouth Duster were missing.

Jane Becker was devastated, but battled through her deepening grief to tell the detectives everything she knew and could remember about the man she knew as Richie, except that she couldn't recall or allow herself to recall his name. "We found her, and the detectives came," Jane Becker said. "I told them right away I knew who killed her, but I couldn't come up with his name. I was so upset, I couldn't think of his name, but I knew it was him." The detectives worried that the victim's mother was too traumatized to assemble an accurate or dependable narrative on what might have happened, especially since some aspects of her description of Judy's relationship with "Richie" didn't add up. They didn't know at the time that Jane Becker had only known the story her daughter had told her, and that the story was fundamentally a lie.

They called their daughter Jane at their home to break the awful news. Jane was horrified, but was also angry and determined enough to insist she would continue to work the phones, as she'd been doing all morning. She was looking for Richie, too. She called the Manhattan Psychiatric Center on Wards Island and asked if he'd come into work that day. There must be some misunderstanding, they told her. Richie—Ricardo Caputo—was not an employee at the Center. He was a patient, and in fact had disappeared three days ago.

The family now knew the dark secret their daughter had been hiding from them for almost a year. To lose a beloved daughter, a loving sister, and now to have to confront this ugly truth! Judy Becker had betrayed her own best interests, and her lifelong habits of honesty and trust, and it had cost her her life. "We were shocked," her sister recalled later, "but at that point everything came together."

Follow-up policework framed the Becker-Caputo relationship in romantic terms, but to this day the Beckers deny that their daughter and Caputo were ever more than just friends. And they angrily dismiss the notion that Judy would ever have influenced Caputo's transfer from Matteawan to Manhattan Psychiatric, saying that she herself had several times expressed misgivings about the transfer.

But in the hours and days after Judy Becker's murder, police faced the task of finding her killer before the trail got cold. They knew where he'd come from —Manhattan Psychiatric—but had no idea where he might have gone after leaving Yonkers. It didn't help that the only photo they had to work with was two years old, or that neighbors in the Odell Avenue building gave inconsistent descriptions of the man they told police they'd seen coming and going from Judy Becker's apartment. The most reliable description was of a man with short dark brown hair and a mustache.

The day after Becker's body had been discovered, police issued an arrest warrant and put out a nation-wide alert. The *Daily News* published Caputo's photo and listed a hot-line number as part of their coverage of the murder. Over one hundred callers contacted the police hot line, people who thought they'd seen the killer since the murder. The calls were local, sug-gesting to police that their man was still in the area. They issued a detailed description of Judy Becker's car, including her Connecticut license plate number "LE 8585." They followed up a lead they never did confirm, that Becker had opened up a joint checking account with Caputo and that one of his first stops after killing her was to wipe out the account to the tune of about two thousand dollars.

Almost from the beginning of the investigation, Yonkers police were in constant contact with their colleagues in Nassau County, who reacted to the murder of Dr. Judy Becker with collective outrage. Detective William Coningsby, who'd participated in the investigation of the Natalie Brown murder nearly three years before, couldn't believe the recent chain of events that put Caputo back on the street and in killing range of other victims.

"Why weren't we called by the mental health peo-ple?" Coningsby fumed. "That's what I wanted to know. That man was never supposed to be *moved* un-less and until we were notified!"

Nassau County Prosecutor Frank Dillon happened to be passing through the Homicide Squad office while Coningsby was raging. As soon as he was filled in on the details, he got on the phone to his boss, District Attorney William Cahn, who immediately scheduled a news conference. Cahn blasted state mental health officials for allowing Caputo to slip through the cracks and, after the press conference, instructed Dillon to get in touch with Harold Brown, Natalie's father, to arrange for security details for the entire Brown family.

For the next two weeks Nassau detectives stood guard twenty-four hours a day over the Brown home and over each member of the Brown family. Caputo was a brutal killer, and now a serial killer. No one was ruling out the possibility that he might return to Long Island and to the Browns, who, in his sick mind, he might see as having been the start of all his troubles.

At the time, Margie Lee Brown was dating Natalie's brother Ed, and though she didn't know the Browns until after Natalie had been murdered, the presence of the detectives and the commotion over Caputo's latest murder and subsequent escape made her feel as though she was reliving Natalie's horrible murder along with the Brown family.

"It made everybody nervous, all over again," she recalled. "When Julie [Natalie's mother] had to go to the store, the detectives went with her. Wherever anyone had to go, the detectives escorted them. Julie had her mother living with her at the time, and if she took her mother to the doctor, one detective went with them and the other stayed behind and watched the house."

Margie remembered one afternoon, the Sunday after the murder, when she and Ed were driving out to eastern Long Island. Suddenly, Ed floored the accelerator and the car rocketed forward.

"What are you doing?" Margie recalls screaming at Ed.

"See that car?" he answered, gesturing ahead of him. "It looks like the car he stole from the Becker girl. I think it matches the description. I'm gonna catch that car and see if it's that S.O.B.!"

Brown raced along the Long Island Expressway, weaving in and out of traffic until he caught up to the bronze-colored Duster. But it wasn't Caputo who stared back at him, terrified.

"I know Ed's not a violent person," Margie Lee recalled, "but to be honest, I didn't know what he would have done if it was that guy. I know he had a special part of him where he kept his feelings about his sister. She was always on his mind."

Natalie Brown was once again on the minds of newspaper editors as well, because her killer was the same suave foreigner who was now linked to Judy Becker's brutal murder. A killer who preys on young women is big news, and a killer set free to kill again is even bigger news.

State mental health officials had their feet held to

the fire, and one official, Dr. Conrad Starace, Deputy Director of the Manhattan Psychiatric Center, seemed to stick both of his feet in his mouth. In an astonishing interview he gave to the *Daily News*, Starace described Ricardo Caputo as a "model patient."

And what about the savage murder of Judy Becker?

"I'm surprised," Starace answered. "He's very good, very well-mannered. He's been missing since Friday, though. He just took off." Starace explained, "We don't have locked wards. He had the freedom to walk around, but he was not supposed to leave the grounds." Starace denied reports based on police sources that Caputo had made it something of a regular habit over the past year to leave the facility to visit Judy Becker at her Yonkers apartment. "He was here all the time, since he was transferred from Matteawan," he said, even going so far as to add, "I don't believe he's the criminal type."

Starace's comments were played and replayed in every subsequent recitation of the story, and pushed the controversy toward the political arena as local elected officials clamored for the spotlight. State Senator Frank Padavan of Queens made headlines by revealing other cases in which certifiably dangerous criminals were placed in nonsecure community-based hospitals and allowed to roam the grounds and the surrounding streets. He cited the case of one man who had been accused—but not convicted at trial—

of decapitating one of his parents, who was later discovered walking around Alley Pond Park in Queens,
free as a bird, near the Creedmoor Psychiatric Center where he'd been transferred several months
earlier.

It would take four more years for the laws to
tighten up and give the courts additional monitoring
authority in the cases of the criminally insane. The
changes, of course, would take place too late for the
Beckers, who were in no mood to wait anyway.

They embarked on their own crusade, starting
with appeals to local television reporters to thoroughly investigate Caputo's transfer to and escape
from the Manhattan Psychiatric Center. Jane Becker,
Judy's mother, wrote first to WABC-TV's ace reporter John Johnson, whose early work on the case
included one report in which he was filmed gaining
access to the facility without anyone stopping him.
She also contacted Geraldo Rivera, fresh from his
award-winning exposé on the scandalous treatment
of patients at the Willowbrook State Hospital on
Staten Island. But neither Rivera nor Johnson chose
to pursue the Caputo story.

Frustrated but undaunted, the Beckers retooled
their efforts to help the Yonkers Police Department in
its continuing investigation. But that effort was also
fruitless. "They were all very nice, very helpful," Jane
Becker recalled. "But they were in Yonkers where
Judy was killed, and he—Caputo—was not in Yonkers." So they went to the FBI and worked with

them, put ads in the papers offering rewards, even the Spanish-language papers. "We did everything we possibly could . . ."

The Beckers even took it upon themselves to follow leads the police judged to be too thin or too remote. They traveled to an antique store in Manhattan that Caputo had supposedly frequented because he knew the proprietors. But Judy's sister Jane says the store owners insisted that Caputo had always been an unwanted guest.

It was a week after the murder when police finally located Judy Becker's car. It had been abandoned on one of the rotting piers jutting out into the Hudson River on the West Side of Manhattan. The speculation was that Caputo might have been trying to lead police into believing he'd escaped on a ship—a claim he would later make about still another escape from authorities hot on his trail. But the car, gone over inch by inch, provided no real clues to Caputo's whereabouts.

Judy Becker's autopsy was conducted at Grasslands Hospital, the same facility where she'd spent a happy year's internship until she began her job at Matteawan State. Her sister Jane recalled how delighted Judy always sounded during the internship, talking animatedly about her work with children. How terribly ironic, Jane remembered, that at the time of her death, Judy was working on an advanced degree at the New School of Social Research in Manhattan and thinking about abandoning her work with the criminally insane to return to helping children.

The Beckers were relentless, but were relentlessly disappointed when their efforts and those of law enforcement failed to run Ricardo Caputo to the ground or explain to anyone's satisfaction how he'd been allowed to draw a beautiful young girl into his killing range.

For a year and a day, at the Manhattan Psychiatric Center, a confessed killer who managed to come off as a "model patient" was given more and more freedom. When he walked away for good, no great fuss was made—"didn't seem like the criminal type," the facility's deputy director said—and three days later the results of his criminal handiwork devastated a family and shocked millions of newspaper readers and television viewers in the New York area.

And, a year later, Jane Becker, who'd never known a moment's respite from the torment unleashed by her daughter's murder, took pen in hand again to write still another series of letters. This time she was contacting police officials in Mexico. A relative had sent her a newspaper clipping: Ricardo Caputo had surfaced again, escaping into Mexico after a jailbreak on the Texas border.

Jane Becker didn't know that Ricardo Caputo had killed again and would kill still again. She only knew that her daughter's killer, an unspeakably cruel killer whose mayhem was an image she would never be able to banish from her mind, had been in the hands of the law—again! And had escaped—*again!*

She wrote with a mother's rage and sorrow, wrote letter after letter, and expected no answers.

CHAPTER SIX

Ricardo Caputo began his life on the run with two murders already under his belt. He may have been in New York City for several days after Judith Becker's murder, supposedly cleaning out the joint checking account she'd opened for the two of them and then ditching her car on a pier on the West Side of Manhattan. But by the time the police traced the car, Caputo was well out of town. He'd gotten used to the notion that the authorities were generally slow to react, starting with the laxity at the Manhattan Psychiatric Center on Wards Island, whose staff had noted his last appearance on October 18 but failed to notify authorities in Nassau County, which had jurisdiction and monitoring authority over his case.

Becker's body wasn't discovered until October 21, and in the first hours, police had to rely on family information to connect the dots. By that time Caputo had slipped through the shadows and zipped out of town, getting as far away from New York as possible. Within two weeks he landed in San Francisco with a new identity but with the same modus operandi. Now he was calling himself Ricardo Dunoguier, and he almost instinctively headed toward the better parts of town where young people with money pursued their genteel lifestyles. He discovered the popular North Beach section, replete with its jumping nightlife, popular restaurants, fine boutiques, and a pleasant blend of pretty homes and sophisticated apartments.

He looked for jobs in his usual lines of work—as a busboy, waiter, or janitor—and told prospective employers and others he met that he was from Uruguay and had most recently been living in Hawaii. The new alias and phony history were the first of many Caputo used along his deadly path. Whatever seemed convenient for the time and place, whatever he thought it would take to convince people, is what he conjured up. In this instance, Caputo thought the image of the mysterious foreigner with some roots close to the West Coast would be helpful in these new surroundings. He worked the area confidently, perhaps believing himself that he was who he claimed. He didn't appear to have a worry in the world about his past or the possibility that he might be caught. People believed his lies and lying was never easier.

It was fall in San Francisco, the weather still mild and the North Beach cafés inviting places for a young man to sit and dream. He'd stroll down bustling Union Street as part of his afternoon routine, grab an outdoor table where he could sit for hours, scout the block and watch the world go by. With no job and plenty of time on his hands, Caputo knew he could blend right into the scene. It would help, he thought, if he had a prop, something that could legitimately occupy his time. It didn't take long before he got himself a sketch pad. He was going to resort to his familiar technique—combining his clever talents and shy charm to make an effective social entrée.

It was early November when Caputo sat himself down at his usual corner table at a favorite Union Street haunt. He was taking in the scene in wide-angle view, and began selecting subjects for his sketch pad. His first choice had been an attractive woman sitting alone at the bar; he sketched away for about fifteen minutes, enough to flesh out her profile, but as he started polishing the sketch, she was joined by friends. Caputo abandoned the project, flipped the page and looked around the café for another subject. His eyes fixed on an attractive brunette at a nearby table whose friend was just saying good-bye. She wore a bulky turtleneck sweater which only partly hid her shapely figure. Her long straight hair and gentle bangs framed a round, pretty face.

Barbara Ann Taylor had stayed behind in the café to finish reading a newspaper, relishing the few minutes she would have to herself. Though only twenty-eight, her position as manager of Contemporary Films, a subsidiary of McGraw-Hill Publishing Company, was a demanding one and kept her extremely busy. She was responsible for the distribution of educational and foreign features, serious material. She was a serious woman who loved her job and didn't mind the long hours. Her rise in the company had been swift, coming only six years after beginning with an entry-level clerk's position following her studies at the University of California in Santa Barbara.

It all made for an overflowing plate she sometimes found difficult to keep in balance, especially since her job as division head required considerable travel both throughout the United States and in Europe. Her initiative knew no bounds; she kept hunting for new challenges, and on this November week she was also starting a new project with a national school association. Her abilities won her constant praise from both her colleagues and her competitors.

Prescott Wright, her peer at rival Macmillan Publications, said flat out that Barbara was "great at her job and great with people. She was intelligent, upwardly mobile, and competent." Wright said she had a regular group of close friends with whom she socialized, often attending concerts or going to the theater. She had little patience for the idle chatter and pickup lines from the bar scene.

Now, stealing a few moments alone with her newspaper, she noticed out of the corner of her eye that a young man seated at a nearby table was looking at her and scribbling away on what appeared to be a sketch pad. She didn't think much of it until she saw him approaching her table.

"I hope you don't mind," he said, his voice melodic and inviting, "but I like to draw and couldn't resist sketching you."

Barbara Taylor put down her newspaper and studied the sketch. "That's really very good," she said, meaning it. "How did you learn how to do that?" Her eyes were wide and curious; she was genuinely surprised.

She didn't know it, but just like the women before her, Barbara Taylor was caught off guard. In her everyday world she was always in charge and in control, her professional and social lives planned and organized. Now, here was someone who came along quite unexpectedly to pleasantly upset the scenario. She was impressed and flattered, and curious to know more about this darkly handsome man with the strong accent and soft voice. After all, he was interesting, and seemed sincerely *interested*.

Caputo, of course, was thrilled to make the connection, and found in Barbara the capacity for the warmth and caring he craved. He also gleaned in that first conversation that she was single, held down a good job, and lived in an upscale San Francisco neighborhood—alone. He didn't tell her that since his arrival in town, he'd been staying in a predictable collection of fleabag hotels, all of them on the east side—the seedy side—of Columbus Street. The nightly rate for his rooms was pretty cheap, but he hadn't landed any work and was running out of cash. Barbara Ann Taylor looked like she had plenty to spare. He showed her one of the other sketches in his pad, a particular favorite of Humphrey Bogart in manly profile. She marveled at its detail, and when he said it was hers to keep, along with the sketch he'd done of her, she smiled warmly.

They shared more stories, laughed easily together, and made plans to see each other again. Soon. By the second week in November, less than a month after Ricardo Caputo had left Judy Becker's lifeless, brutalized body on her bed in Yonkers, he was in another bed with another woman a continent away. When Barbara Taylor invited him to move in while he looked for work, he didn't waste a minute before grabbing the most convenient living arrangement possible. She paid the bills and provided the roof, while he supposedly searched for that ever-elusive job.

Taylor made her home in a well-kept prewar building in exclusive Pacific Heights. Her two-bedroom apartment at 2041 Broadway was listed as #3, even though it was on the first living level. There were garages below and four apartments above. Plenty of privacy, comfort and style, just the way Barbara liked it—and the way the young man who called himself Ricardo Dunoguier liked it as well.

The relationship continued through the holidays. In late December Barbara brought Caputo to her parents' home in Fremont, across San Francisco Bay, to meet the family, which consisted of her father Judson, the retired and well-respected principal of James Logan High School in Union City, her mother Vera, and her thirty-one-year-old sister Susan, who was a traffic manager for a food company. The Taylor family greeted Caputo warmly, convinced, they said later, that he was a serious man who was obviously very much in love with Barbara.

It was happening again, though Caputo/Dunoguier told himself again and again that this time it was love, this time it would last, this time he'd found the answer. An outsider would surely have seen the pattern, and perhaps without even knowing it, Caputo was laying the groundwork for the same scenario. It's as if he had an eerie knack for finding accomplished women who, despite their close-knit families, maintained their spirit of independence and adventure. It was that spirit that allowed them to invite the stranger into their lives; the fact that their parents always seemed to like him helped them defeat their better judgment and drown out their doubts. In short order, and it always happened quickly, the stranger insinuated himself into their lives—one life at a time—without much more to offer than his ultimately deadly charm. And it worked for him again and again.

Perhaps, like other women who'd been involved with Caputo, Barbara Taylor harbored her own troubling suspicions and for that reason said little to her friends about him. Her colleagues did see him when he stopped by her office, and would later say they thought the two of them a most unlikely couple. But they trusted Barbara's judgment and wanted her to be happy.

Throughout the holiday season of 1974–75, Ricardo Caputo could not have had it any better. He was living well; Barbara was extremely generous, picking up all the bills and expenses and rarely questioning him on his job search. And she didn't skimp on gifts. When they planned an outing together, she bought him a pair of expensive brown suede hiking boots, the top-of-the-line model with metal-reinforced heels. The kind he said he'd always wanted.

But as the calendar turned past the new year, Barbara began noticing that the bills were beginning to pile up. She finally began pressing Ricardo about getting a job, and began losing patience with his increasingly lame excuses. One of his acquaintances, a local man named Domingo Giuffra, said later that Caputo admitted to him that he was "a gigolo" and that Barbara Taylor was his ticket away from poverty. He boasted to Giuffra that Barbara had recently signed a hefty contract to work as a consultant for a series of television shows, and that he was expecting his good life to get even better.

But by early March, Barbara had other ideas. Her life was complicated now, as she was in the process of closing up her San Francisco office because her job was relocating to Chicago. Whether she'd definitely decided to move to Chicago was never clear, say her friends; what was clear was that she wanted Ricardo to relocate right out of her life. She knew it would be a difficult job to convince him to leave, and she began to think about how best to get it done. Despite his cavalier boasts to friends, he was still telling Barbara how much he loved her and that his intentions were serious. But she was beginning to wonder what his intentions really were. He seemed a stranger again, a stranger she wanted out of her bed, out of her apartment, and out of her life for good. As March progressed, she pondered her options for ending the relationship. He wasn't taking hints. And she wanted it to end for another reason; she had begun dating someone else.

One day she hit on a plan. Ricardo had often talked about Hawaii and claimed he wanted one day to return there to work. The cost of a plane ticket might just do it, Barbara thought, and she put in a call to her travel agent.

"Ricardo," she said one night, the ticket in an envelope in her hand. "I know this is something you've been talking about for some time. I really wanted to do this for you, and I hope you like it. Here . . ."

Caputo opened the envelope and saw the ticket. Just one ticket.

"Aren't you going to come with me?" he asked, both hurt and suspicious.

"I can't," Barbara lied. "I wanted to, but I have too much work to do. Besides, I'll see you when you get back." She was in fact hoping he would stay in Hawaii, perhaps latch on to someone else, and just cash in the return ticket. If this is an investment, she thought, I hope it's worth it.

Caputo pocketed the ticket.

* * *

He wasn't going to allow himself to get too upset. Here he was with a ticket to the tropical paradise he'd always dreamed of visiting—though he'd told many people he met in San Francisco that he'd lived and worked in Hawaii before landing in California. He figured he'd find some sun and fun on the islands. And now at least he wouldn't be lying when he told people he lived there. Not that Ricardo Caputo ever cared about when he was lying or who he was lying to. He'd worry about Barbara's motives later, and when he got back, he'd turn the charm up another notch if he had to, aided by what would surely be a lustrous tan, and win her over for good. He wasn't worried. This one was different. This time it would be different.

On the plane, he looked down at the sparkling blue Pacific Ocean and let all the doubts drift right out of his head. Two weeks on Hawaii's beautiful beaches, with all those glistening bodies. His mind was filled with possibilities and daydreams of limitless pleasure.

CHAPTER SEVEN

It was called Blue Hawaii and it was one of the most popular hangouts for young people in all of Honolulu. Through a local agency called A-One Employment, Ricardo Caputo snagged a busboy's job working the dinner shift by night, allowing him plenty of beach time by day.

His trim body, getting tanner with each passing day, and his obvious skills at swimming and casual conversation, suited him just perfectly for the sandy social scene. He began wearing sleek new wraparound sunglasses, which heightened his self-image as a suave and engaging newcomer who, with the fascinating stories that rolled off his tongue, would make him a welcome addition to any group. Quite predictably, the women were cozying up to this attractive package, and Caputo wasn't ignoring their attentions. He was especially drawn to one young woman he met on the beach, whose name, coincidentally, he thought, was Barbara. This Barbara was a student, and, she later told police, Caputo pursued her in a manner far different than the light flirtation she'd had in mind.

On Wednesday, March 26, she told police, Ricardo Caputo took her to his room, beat and raped her, only ending his assault when his temporary roommate heard the commotion as he approached the room and banged on the door. Barbara fled, but did not call the police right away. Instead she waited a day and tried to find her attacker, to confront him—publicly—but he was nowhere to be found. When she later gave a full statement to the authorities, she recalled one aspect of her attacker's appearance in vivid detail. It was unusual in a tropical paradise for someone to be wearing heavy brown suede hiking boots. She said she'd recognize the boots right away, because they had steel-reinforced heels.

Caputo knew he was in trouble, and he didn't want to stick around for the consequences. Once again the problem of crossed intentions and subsequent rejection reared its ugly head. Once again the rage turned to violence, and once again Caputo decided to cut and run. He hopped the first available flight back to California, a red-eye that touched down in San Francisco just before ten A.M. Thursday, March 27. Barbara Taylor was in her office when the phone rang.

"Hi, Barbara? It's Ricardo." He listened as she said nothing. "I missed you so much, I had to come back early to see you. Do you think you could come and pick me up at the airport?"

Barbara stifled a gasp and twisted the telephone cord while her mind raced. He wasn't supposed to be back until Sunday, if he was going to come back at all!

Why was he back so soon? What am I going to do with him? she thought. Why can't he just leave me alone!

What she said into the phone was, "Sure, I'll come get you. How was Hawaii?"

"Oh, it was great," he said. "I'll tell you all about it when I see you."

Barbara hung up the phone and expelled several deep breaths, taking off her black-framed glasses and rubbing her eyes. A colleague, William Taylor, looked in on her just then and noticed the somber, concerned look on her face. He was one of Barbara's good friends, and said then that he was worried about her. She told him and other co-workers that Ricardo had returned unexpectedly and that she was going to fetch him at the airport and then return to work.

By noon she was back in her office, explaining that Ricardo seemed to be exhausted and wanted simply to go to her apartment and catch up on sleep.

But Barbara, staring at the pile of papers sitting on her desktop awaiting her attention, knew that concentrating on work would be a losing battle. She was distracted, she was angry. And she was confused about how to deal with another dilemma that hadn't existed a few hours ago. She had a date that night, with the man she'd been seeing, a man who'd become very important to her. She slumped down into her plush executive's chair and then steeled herself for a phone call she hated to make.

"Hi, John? It's Barbara."

John Weber heard the strain in her voice. "How are you, what's the matter?" he asked cautiously.

"Listen, this is something I have to tell you, and please don't be upset," she said, her words a torrent. "Ricardo came back from Hawaii today, he's at my apartment. I know I shouldn't have brought him back there, and I planned for him never to stay there again, but he was insistent, saying he missed me and all that and that he just wanted to get some sleep. I don't think I'm going to be able to see you tonight because he'll get upset. But I'm going to tell him that it's over. I care about you very much, John, and I want you to know that. Just be patient with me, I can handle this. I'm trying to handle this the best way I can . . ."

John Weber didn't like what he was hearing, and he was frustrated as he'd always been whenever the subject of Ricardo came up, because he realized there was little he could do. He and Barbara had started dating a few months before and had hit it off right from the start, and while he was sure her relationship with this Ricardo character was on the downswing, it seemed to be dragging on and on. He believed Barbara was serious about breaking it off, but also knew there was nothing he could do or say to help her get it done any more quickly. He was just going to have to wait, one more night, she was saying; one final conversation and she'd have Ricardo out of her hair.

It was a horrible phone call that left Barbara Taylor

totally frazzled. Unable to work, she dialed her sister Susan for some advice, some sympathy, and some cheering up, if that were even possible. The worst thing of all, she told Susan, was that Ricardo kept saying during the ride from the airport that he wanted to marry her! He didn't have a clue that marriage to him was the furthest thing from her mind; he had no grasp of reality, and it was unsettling. Maybe even a little frightening. And now she had to tell him in no uncertain terms that it was over completely between them.

Just be honest, Susan said, and everything will work out fine. Barbara wasn't sure about that, not sure at all, but she quickly turned to a more pleasant topic, the coming weekend's Easter Sunday dinner at their parents' home.

"We'll see each other then," Barbara said, relief in her voice, and perhaps even a hint of pleasure at the thought of being with her family. "Sunday, then. Can't wait . . ."

Neighbors said that later that Thursday night, Holy Thursday night, they heard two people arguing vehemently in Barbara Taylor's apartment.

The next morning, on Good Friday, Barbara walked the six blocks to Café Malvina on Grant Avenue. She was a regular customer there, stopping in several times a week in the morning on her way to work, grabbing a cappuccino, and taking a quick read of the paper. She stayed for about an hour this time, seemingly alone with troubling thoughts and perhaps even fears. She felt alone and lonely, and finally returned home to make some phone calls. She reached one friend, Chuck Ziegler, and talked to him for about fifteen minutes. Only the police know what they discussed. But apparently it was the last phone call Barbara Taylor ever made.

About an hour later a man fitting the description of an illegal immigrant who called himself Ricardo Dunoguier was seen leaving Barbara Taylor's apartment building with a suitcase in one hand. A witness, Thomas Griggs, later told police he recognized him as the same man who carried the same suitcase into Barbara's place the day before.

The all-too-familiar and deadly pattern had once again come full circle. And it would be another two days before the carnage of the killer was—once again —discovered by another victim's family.

CHAPTER EIGHT

Easter Sunday dinner sat on the table far too long in the Taylor home. It grew cold, matching the chill that ran down the family's collective spine. They all knew Barbara was coming home for the weekend and that she was looking forward to the holiday gathering. They knew too that not even the turmoil in her personal life could have kept her from coming.

Judson Taylor grew more and more anxious each time he called his daughter's apartment and got no answer. He was a man of action, not the kind to sit around and wonder and worry, so he got into his car and drove to her apartment. He pulled up in front of the building and stopped at the foot of her driveway, noticing with a start that her car was in the garage beneath her apartment. Taylor now ruled out the possibility he'd feared—that something had happened to his daughter on the road—but the other possibilities that flooded his mind were equally disturbing. If she was home, upstairs in her apartment, she surely would have phoned her family. Taylor tried to keep his feelings of dread at bay as he scaled her fire escape to see if anything was visible through her windows. The curtains were drawn, but the lights were on. But Judson Taylor heard not a sound. No music, no talking, no movement. If he was looking for clues, any clue, that his daughter might still be all right, the stillness of the apartment wasn't giving anything up. Taylor clambered back down the fire escape and called the police.

When they arrived, they retraced Taylor's route up the fire escape and simply pried open the window. They went inside, Judson Taylor following, and the mystery of Barbara Taylor's whereabouts was solved in the cruelest instant a parent could ever know.

The apartment was thick with the smell of death. Barbara's bedroom was a frightful scene, her usually neat desktop ravaged by an apparently frantic search, and all of her bureau drawers rifled. Papers and clothing were tossed all over the place. The corner of an electric blanket remained on the bed, but the rest had been pulled off to the floor on the far side. When the police officers taking their first look at the crime scene stepped around the bed, they had to avoid a large pool of blood. The blood had poured from Barbara Taylor's nude body, covered by the electric blanket which her killer had left switched on. Her head had been bashed in. Underneath Barbara Taylor's body police found a blood-soaked brown suede boot with leather laces and steel-reinforced heels. The boot's mate was in the bedroom closet.

Barbara Taylor had been stomped to death. The autopsy revealed that the four deep lacerations to her head were made by the heel of the brown suede boot. Yes, confirmed Barbara's colleague William Taylor, they were the same boots Ricardo Dunoguier had worn every time he'd seen him. Forensic tests proved the blood on the boot was Barbara Taylor's blood, and suggested because of the amount of bleeding from each wound that the blows might have been administered over a period of ten to fifteen minutes. Ten to fifteen minutes of deliberate, killing rage.

San Francisco Police Inspector Earl Sanders caught the case, and like the counterparts he didn't yet know he had in Yonkers, New York, soon found himself chasing a shadow seen by many but truly known to no one. His investigators built the best file they could on one Ricardo Dunoguier, who Sanders said became "increasingly conspicuous by his absence." But there wasn't much to go on besides witness accounts from those who'd met him through Barbara Taylor. For days the portfolio of the killer's past that could be put together began and ended with Ricardo's association with his victim, and, of course, he was nowhere to be found.

But if Caputo had ransacked his latest victim's apartment in hopes of removing any trace of his identity, he overlooked one crucial item—a roll of film that was still in Barbara's camera. When police developed the film, they came up with a half-dozen photos of Caputo, posing and preening in all his glory. In one of the shots he was wearing the suede work boots. Sanders had the photos reproduced and shown all around town, but the mass canvassing only confirmed that the man in the photos had spent time in a few flophouses before taking up with his victim. No one had a story that checked out about where he'd come from or, more importantly, where he might have fled to now. The cops ran down the oft-repeated story Caputo had told about his origins in Uruguay and hit one dead end after another. Sanders ran down every lead emanating from Caputo's trip to Hawaii, but since his rape victim hadn't yet reported his assault, the Hawaii leads resulted only in more of the same: a whisper of a man who'd charmed his way through his chosen social set, whose alias-of-the-moment and fabrication of a life allowed him to slip back into invisibility whenever he chose. For days Inspector Sanders searched in vain for this invisible man named Ricardo Dunoguier, never knowing that his prey had a history that confirmed him as a monster, not knowing that the monster's real name was Ricardo Silvio Caputo. Until the fingerprint checks came back, Sanders hadn't the vaguest notion that his killer had killed before with equivalent brutality, had escaped from a mental institution and was already the object of a nationwide search. And the fingerprint checks didn't come from the crime scene in Barbara Taylor's apartment. They came in nearly ten days later when Caputo, on the run again, once again slipped in and out of the grasp of the authorities. As Barbara Taylor's family and friends grieved her loss, still numb in the present emotions of shock and distress, Ricardo Dunoguier was already hundreds of miles away and no doubt calculating his future. He knew the routine all too well from previous experience: the hasty retreat from Hawaii just several weeks before, the escape from New York six months ago after Judy Becker's murder. This time he decided to leave the United States altogether. He traveled nearly a thousand miles south to the Mexican border. He'd slip in unnoticed, he believed, and lose himself in the Latin culture into which he could easily assimilate. First he had to choose another alias, and come up with papers to support his latest phony identity. He settled on the name Ricardo Pinto, and would claim he was a Mexican citizen who was just returning home.

But when the shadow reached the border, he was suddenly very visible and his real identity very much in peril of discovery. The alias he'd chosen, with its casually attached fabricated history, was about to betray him.

CHAPTER NINE

Ricardo Caputo stayed on the ground, and low to the ground, since fleeing San Francisco. He knew enough to avoid airports and train stations, and knew from his past wanderings that the road could be his friend as long as he stayed on the move. He was getting used to the new name that he'd chosen, getting used to the idea that he could shed one identity for a new one as though he was merely changing a shirt. Let's see, should he shave off his mustache or trim his hair? He contemplated putting on a lot of weight and thought that at some point it might be a good idea.

But choosing a Mexican identity turned out to be one of his closest calls. Barbara Taylor had been dead for just three days when the young man carrying papers saying he was Ricardo Pinto arrived in El Paso, a border town in southwest Texas where three bridges spanned the Rio Grande into Mexico. Logically, the northernmost bridge was called the Paso Del Norte, followed as the river flowed to the south by the Bridge of the Americas and, finally, the Ysleta port of entry in the south.

Caputo/Pinto took his shot at the first available

span, crossing the bridge calmly and handing his papers over to the two Mexican Federales who saw nothing suspicious in his appearance. They quickly glanced at his papers and were about to hand them back to him and wave him on when his confident answers to their few curt questions set off their internal alarms. The Federales looked at each other and nodded imperceptibly: Señor Pinto's accent was wrong, and fell in the rhythms and expressions that were most assuredly not Mexican! He'd blown his cover. Thinking quickly but battling his rising panic, Caputo offered another alibi, claiming he was an Argentinean stowaway who'd arrived in the United States a few days before on a ship that was docked in Miami. Save it for the American feds, the Mexican officials told him as they handed him over.

Ricardo Caputo had been a few steps and a few ill-chosen spoken words away from long-term freedom, and now he found himself being marched back toward the El Paso Detention Facility for Illegal Immigrants. He knew what to expect there: more questions, and a background check. He was taken to the service processing center and run through the standard booking procedure. His mind raced: he'd been able to change his name, his background, even his appearance, but there was one thing that always remained the same—his fingerprints. As he saw the inked images of his prints pressed to the standard form, he knew he was in dire straits. In a few days at most, the prints would trigger all kinds of alerts at several levels of the criminal justice system. After the prints were matched, the torrent of warrants would be sent through to the usually sleepy detention center, and Ricardo Caputo's flight to freedom would come to a crashing end. A veritable army of law enforcement types, led by the FBI, would be followed by legions of reporters and photographers who would turn the somber-looking detention center, and the crossing with the sun-face logo in sombrero and cowboy boots beneath the slogan "Hasta La Vista," into the most visible images on the evening news and on the front pages of newspapers across the land. Caputo, sitting glumly on his assigned cot in one of the two dorms in the center, knew what would happen, and knew with absolute certainty that if he didn't do something, and quickly, he would never taste freedom again.

He ignored his sparse surroundings and all but a few of his fellow inmates. He carefully cultivated those few, offering friendship and a few hints of conspiracy.

The FBI came calling the next day but still didn't have the fingerprint match that would have told them the whole story. It was Thursday morning, April 4, and the agents made the trip to El Paso only because they had jurisdiction for crimes on the high seas and they wanted to evaluate prisoner Pinto's stowaway claim. He repeated his dramatic tale of illegal entry from South America but then refused to say more, demanding an attorney. The agents sighed at the standard ploy but knew they were powerless to force any further statements. They told the prisoner they'd return in a week, on April 11, and by then would have checked out his story thoroughly. He wasn't going anywhere anyway, they knew—or at least thought.

Ricardo Caputo couldn't have had better news. He knew the clock was ticking and the fingerprint check could come back at any time, but as he watched the agents bid good-bye to the border guards, he knew he had the authorities off his back, at least for a little while longer.

As Caputo resettled in his dorm, breathing sighs of relief, the relatives and friends of Barbara Taylor were making their way to 255 H Street in Fremont, California. There, at the Niles Congregational Church, they would pay their last respects and say good-bye at her funeral service. No one in the church, and no one on the stymied investigative team had any idea that morning that Barbara's killer was in custody a thousand miles away. They didn't know it in El Paso either, until it was too late. No one knew, that is, except one man.

He'd caught a break and wasn't going to waste it. Back in the dorm, he pressed his friendship upon the fellow detainees he'd determined might help him hatch his plot. One was a Canadian, another a resident of Belize, a third from British Honduras. Escape was the only way out. Caputo was going to need help, from the clock and from his newfound friends.

* * *

It was two A.M. on Monday morning, April 8. Amazingly, the fingerprint check on the prisoner who called himself Ricardo Pinto still hadn't come back. On that morning Detention Officer Michael Guerrero was a quarter of the way through his graveyard shift, having relieved colleague Jesus Vela two hours earlier. He took his post and sat at a simple wooden chair behind a metal desk in the middle of one of the dorms. Only one guard was scheduled to supervise the night shift in each dorm, the facility rated for minimum security despite its capacity for up to four hundred prisoners. The dorms were unconnected to the mess hall and the recreation area, and the administrative offices were situated outside the high-security fences that ringed the complex.

Guerrero was uneasy as his shift progressed. It was usually drudge work, babysitting, but he was aware that several of the detainees seemed unusually restless.

"I noticed there was something wrong," he recalled. "The same people kept getting up from their cots, going to the bathroom or going to have a cigarette. They were talking to each other, but I didn't quite know what to make of it."

He would soon know exactly what to make of it.

The prisoner called Pinto was ready to make his move. He approached Guerrero slowly, casually.

"Officer," he said in his small, unthreatening voice, "I have a headache. Do you have any aspirin?"

The veteran guard started rummaging through his desk drawer. As he searched the drawers' contents, Caputo pulled out a large kitchen knife one of his cohorts had spirited during his working shift in the mess kitchen.

Caputo moved swiftly, grabbing the burlier guard from behind and holding the knife to his neck. Now his voice changed and was purely threatening.

"We're going out one way or the other, and this is the way it's gonna be," he said ominously. He pressed the knife blade more insistently into Guerrero's neck. "You might as well cooperate and make it easy on yourself."

Guerrero gulped hard. "No problem," he said, knowing he had no choice at this point. He wasn't armed; none of the interior guards at the facility carried weapons, only walkie-talkies. Caputo had thought his plan through, and now reached for the radio, grabbing it off the officer's desk and thereby cutting him off from any chance at calling for help. Caputo's team surrounded the guard while the rest of the detainees remained on their cots, most feigning sleep. They either knew about the plot and cooperated by not interfering or simply wanted to stay out of it and the added trouble it likely promised.

Caputo now shoved the officer into movement, holding the knife to his neck the whole time while his cohorts followed. The procession lurched down the corridor toward the dorm's front doors. Guerrero, of course, had the keys to open all the doors in the facil-

ity. There was a short detour to the kitchen so
Caputo's team could procure other weapons. When
one of the men came out happily brandishing a meat
cleaver Guerrero became truly frightened for the
first time. He recalled thinking, "That thing could
chop somebody's head off. And one of these guys
could do it!"

The group moved outside the mess hall, heading
toward the front gate that separated them from the
main control room. Guerrero explained that he
didn't have a key to the gate, it had to be opened
electronically by one of the three officers stationed in
the control room to monitor the rest of the camp.

Caputo shoved Guerrero hard, tightening his grip
even as he pressed the officer into the bright lights
that illuminated the area surrounding the main gate.

"I'm holding one of your officers," he shouted,
knowing he could be heard. "We're gonna be taking
off, and if you don't want anything to happen to him,
open the gate right now!" Caputo, who knew he was
being watched, slashed the knife blade quickly but
not too deeply across Guerrero's neck. The inch-long
gash drew blood, and Guerrero grew frantic. "I said
to myself, 'This is it.' In a few seconds, maybe a few
minutes, my entire life went past my mind, like they
say. I was thinking of my family. I had the feeling, I
was certain, I wasn't going to come out of this
alive . . ."

But the control room guards knew the escaping
inmates were desperate and meant business. They let

the gate slide open, and Caputo and his cohorts rushed inside. When the gate to the outside swung open, the escapees made one more detour—"They knew exactly where to go to take money and additional weapons," Guerrero said. They headed for the safe in the administrative office outside the complex. There they grabbed around two thousand dollars in American currency and some 3100 pesos, money that had been surrendered by the detainees upon their incarceration. They also came away with three .38 caliber revolvers, though they couldn't find the ammunition to go with the weapons.

There was one final detail in the plan Caputo had envisioned and now had nearly carried out.

Squeezing Guerrero with sudden ferocity, he demanded the guard's car keys. Guerrero sifted through his trouser pockets and handed over the keys to his 1971 blue and white Chevy Impala. The group moved quickly but awkwardly to the parking lot, one of them shouting, "Let's take the guard with us! We can make him drive, and if he's any trouble we can get rid of him later!" But Caputo wanted none of that plan, hollering back, "I'm in charge, and he's not going anywhere." But Caputo, energized by his success so far and now making it up as he went along, instructed his team excitedly, "We're going back to the cells." They retraced their steps and headed toward the control room that led to the camp's few maximum security cells, using their hold on Guerrero and the guns only they knew were unloaded to force the other on-duty officers into their own prison cells, where they were quickly locked up. They then left at their leisure, piling into the Chevy.

The daring escape was the big headline in all the local papers the next day, running across the top of both the *El Paso Herald Post* and the *El Paso Times*. But before the day was out, the banner headlines would be supplanted by an even bigger story.

Ricardo Pinto's fingerprints came back, matched to the name of a serial killer whose real name was Ricardo Caputo. Police officials from Long Island to Yonkers to San Francisco, where Inspector Sanders's team had quickly put the story together, were burning up the phone lines trying to find out what the hell had happened in El Paso. They'd had him, the FBI had sent agents to question him, and all they'd come away with was some lame story from the prisoner about how he smuggled himself into America by stowing away on a ship! What was more frustrating was that Nassau County authorities claimed they had received a phone call while Caputo was still incarcerated there; apparently, some early paperwork had come back on their detainee and the federal officials were checking him out. Are you looking for this guy? they wanted to know. Detective William Coningsby and Prosecutor Frank Dillon remember the phone call, and also recall telling the authorities that this guy was dangerous. But the warning came too late. Within hours, Caputo had carried out his escape.

Yet another arrest warrant was readied in San

Francisco, this time under the alias Caputo had used in that city. Warrant #176281 of 1985 charged Ricardo Dunoguier with murder, stating in specific:

> The People of the State of California, to any peace officer of this state: COMPLAINT upon oath having been made this day before me that the offense is the felony, to wit: Violation of Section 187 of the California Penal Code has been committed, and this instrument accuses Ricardo Dunoguier thereof. You are hereby commanded forthwith to arrest the above-named defendant and bring him forthwith before the Municipal Court of the City and County of San Francisco, State of California . . .

In his own handwriting the judge issuing the warrant had written the words, "No Bail."

In short order the San Francisco Police Department also applied for and received what's called a UFAP warrant—the acronym stands for the words "Unlawful Flight from Prosecution," and the special warrant committed the FBI to the search. Not that the bureau needed to be brought into the case by local cops in San Francisco; after all, the bureau's own agents had had Ricardo Caputo in their sights, in their custody, in a locked facility, and had unwittingly given him the one chance he needed to hatch his escape plan. The UFAP warrant did provide some information that seemed vaguely amusing—information based on interviews with the suspect's acquaintances in California and Hawaii, his two most recent stops before heading to El Paso—suggesting that his likely destinations would have to include New York, Florida, Nevada . . . or China!

In El Paso, meanwhile, local warrants were issued charging Caputo with the additional crimes of assault on a federal officer, escape from prison, and theft of government property.

Within days, two of the three detainees who'd escaped with Caputo were back in federal custody. One was found hiding in a hotel in Juarez, Mexico. Another was caught in a store trying to use a credit card stolen from one of the officers at the detention camp.

Guerrero's 1971 Chevy Impala was recovered but the third detainee was never found. And Ricardo Caputo, the big fish and the one that got away, again, was in the Mexican wind, invisible again, the ladykiller-turned-shadow one more time.

CHAPTER TEN

Mexico was easy, just the right place to hide, and Ricardo Caputo made certain to burrow deep into the sprawling rough country a thousand miles south of the U.S. border to teeming Mexico City. He knew that north of the border, authorities throughout the United States had awakened fully to the realization that a multiple killer, and a vicious killer at that, was on the loose and that they'd failed twice to hold him when he was in their grasp. But the Mexican capital city, with its shoulder-to-shoulder population of nine million and its scores of faceless barrios, was a perfect fit for a man who spoke the language, had a flair for easy conversation and a need to stay out of the reach of the long arm of American law.

He'd already decided on still another name change, this time selecting Ricardo Martinez Diaz. The American authorities could press their search all they wanted, he guessed; he was leaving no paper trail, he was invisible again. The Americans had even appealed for help to Interpol, the coordinating agency for law enforcement agencies around the world, but even Interpol needed something to go on, and the elusive Caputo was determined to give them nothing. The search to the north stalled; leads had dried up or turned out to be undependable. As Caputo blended ever more thoroughly into his new surroundings, picking up menial odd jobs at first and keeping his human contacts casual, his confidence returned. He'd proven his ability once again to slip through the cracks in desperate circumstances.

Within months of his escape from El Paso's detention center, Caputo had settled in Coyoacan, a middle-class neighborhood in the south-central section of Mexico City. He moved into a pleasant garden apartment complex on Avenida Coyoacan 334 in a community known as Colonia del Valle. While some of the apartments looked out on the pretty central courtyard, Caputo's unit, number 4, faced the street. Coyoacan's location appealed to Caputo's returning need to plug into the best and most exciting locations wherever he lived. His apartment was convenient to the city's majestic cultural and educational institutions, including the deservedly famous Universidad Nacional Autonoma de Mexico, which was a mere two miles by bus from his door. The breathtaking buildings of what was called University City contained much artwork of note, including murals by modern master Diego Rivera. Also within shouting distance of Caputo's new home was the Bosque de Chapultepec, the largest and most exquisite of the city's many parks, encompassing more than a thousand acres. On its grounds were several separate zoos, many manicured gardens, and a number of the city's thirty-five museums. The park was a natural draw for the young dreamer from the Coyoacan, who found himself spending more and more time exploring its wonders.

Jesus Vela was also drawn to the cultural delights of Mexico City. When the young Mexican-American and his wife finally carved out room for a long-awaited extended vacation, Mexico City was their chosen destination. It was 1976, a year after Vela and three other detention officers were held hostage by a man who then called himself Ricardo Pinto. But it had been fifteen years since he'd been back to the country of his birth, and he and his wife excitedly pored over the guidebooks as they planned their trips. His vacation was occupying all his thoughts; and the issue of Ricardo Pinto was the furthest thing from his mind.

When the Velas were settled after their trip to Mexico City, one of their first stops was to the Museo Nacional de Antropologia—the Anthropology Museum—in the Bosque de Chapultepec. The museum was celebrated in all the guidebooks for its exhibits and artifacts depicting the country's ancient civilizations.

The couple arrived at the museum just as one of the morning's first tours was getting under way. One of the museum's guards noticed the Velas in an animated discussion—apparently, he deduced, they were debating whether to join the tour. On his own initiative, the guard approached the tour guide and inquired as to whether he'd mind adding two more people to the group. The guide looked toward the couple and said something to the security guard, who then approached the Velas.

"This tour guide says he knows you," he said to Jesus Vela. "He's curious about where he's seen you before. Do you and your wife want to join the group?"

But Vela was confused, momentarily off balance. He didn't know anybody in Mexico City and certainly didn't believe he'd ever have run into someone who was a museum tour guide here. He looked over at the guide, who'd momentarily turned his attention to a questioner in his group, and said, half aloud, "No . . . I don't think so. I don't know him."

But they changed their minds and decided to tag along for the tour anyway. As they made the rounds of the exhibits, Vela noticed that the guide kept sneaking looks his way, as though still trying to place his face. Finally, during a pause in the group's circuit, the guide approached him.

"I know you from somewhere," he said, his accent not quite right for Mexico City. Now Vela peered more closely at the guide; something about him, about his voice particularly, was off-putting. His manner seemed at odds with his position, just seemed out of whack. Vela's instincts as a prison guard kicked in; something about this guy didn't add up, though he couldn't put his finger on it. Play it safe, his instincts told him, throw him a curve, maybe, and reveal little.

"I'm from the Bay area, San Francisco," he lied, surprised at the reaction his lie received. Without warning the tour guide ended the exchange, seeming to have suddenly lost interest in any further conversation. He withdrew to the group, instructing them pleasantly that it was time to move along.

But just before he'd turned back toward the group, Vela had taken a close look at the photograph on the guide's identification badge. He was jolted by a shock of recognition.

"That's when I knew exactly who I'd been talking to," Vela explained later. In person the guide had a receding hairline and a pencil-thin mustache. The photo was from an earlier time, perhaps only months earlier but showing a man whose appearance was distinctly familiar to Jesus Vela.

"There was no mistaking it," Vela recalled. "It was the man I'd known as Ricardo Pinto. The guy who'd escaped, who'd threatened my life. I got goose pimples all over as I realized it was him. My wife and I got out of there and, first chance I got, I called the FBI. I don't know what happened after that."

What happened was that nothing happened. Caputo had been taken aback by Vela's mention of San Francisco, but he never did put it together that Vela had been one of his hostages in El Paso. He would have remembered Mike Guerrero, whose neck he'd slashed and whose torso he'd held in his desperate grip during the long moments of the escape; but Jesus Vela was just one of the bit players that early morning, someone whose appearance never registered.

Yes, Caputo had had a moment's anxiety during his conversation with Vela, but it had dissipated quickly and he'd returned to his routines, remaining in the tour guide's job he enjoyed, even though it was work that kept him very much in the public eye. The rest of his life was comfortable, familiar; all it lacked, in fact, was the presence of a woman. It was inevitable that he'd meet that woman, and that like her predecessors, she'd be swept under by his persuasive charm.

Her name was Laura Maria Gomez Saenz, a beautiful twenty-five-year-old brunette from a wealthy local family who was a student at the University of Mexico. How and under what circumstances she'd been wooed and won by the man known in Coyoacan as Ricardo Martinez Diaz were never known. What did become known, to the shock and horror of another city in another country, was how Laura Gomez died.

It was October 3, 1977, when police were summoned by a panicked neighbor's phone call to apartment number four at the Colonia del Valle. What they discovered was so physically repellent, they found themselves recoiling in horror at the same time knowing they had to proceed. The apartment was hot, overheated, and the stench of death was nauseating. The bloodied body of a young woman was lying face down on the bed, wearing only panties and the evidence that a killer of inexplicable, inhuman cruelty had snuffed out her life.

The apartment around the body was in chaos, as though a sudden violent storm had blown through. There was blood everywhere, evidence of a terrible, protracted struggle of some sort. Clothes and papers had piled up on every available surface; there were several empty liquor bottles in a filthy cluttered kitchen. As the officers walked around gingerly, they looked down and noticed that the victim's blood had pooled in several places. They wondered, in amazement and disgust: had her killer dragged her through the entire apartment, stopping at several points to administer more torture?

And torture seemed to have been on his mind at least as much as murder. The completed autopsy report revealed the work of a killer of truly boundless rage. His victim had suffered no fewer than ten deep contusions likely to have been caused by blows from "a pipelike object." One of the blows to the back of her head was whipped with such force that two of her teeth had been knocked out, though a news account following the release of the autopsy results suggested the possibility that the killer had pulled her teeth out with a pair of available pliers. The news report also said the killer might have forced his victim to drink industrial alcohol, which was found in her system, before she died. The autopsy added that at the time of her death, Laura Maria Gomez Saenz was two months pregnant. There was further speculation that she was carrying her killer's child and that news of her pregnancy might have launched him into his lethal rage.

The crime scene investigation also suggested another chilling detail: with time of death having been established to a reasonable degree of certainty, it was possible the killer, his explosion having passed, and leaving awful mayhem in its wake, might have stayed at the apartment for a while; shaving, washing up, making himself a cup of coffee, scanning a newspaper. The official cause of death—trauma to the facial skull—was hardly adequate to describe the ending of Laura Gomez's life. Dr. Ramon Fernandez Perez, General Director of Mexico City's Medical Forensic Service, reviewed the entire autopsy report before announcing to reporters, "This killer . . . is a beast."

Once again the homicide detectives investigating a murder committed by Ricardo Caputo would be stymied. Neighbors in the apartment complex couldn't recall hearing or seeing anything unusual in the days before Laura Gomez was killed. One neighbor, a man named José Serafin Misreja, had only moved into his apartment the week before the murder. He did tell police he'd seen a man fitting Caputo's description coming and going from apartment number four all that week, but that's all he offered.

In fact, while the police investigation got them nowhere in their search for the killer, it did reveal a bit about how Caputo, under the name Ricardo Martinez Diaz, had lived in Mexico for the past two years. It was possible, for example, that he'd married in Mexico before taking up with Laura Gomez. Rent and electric bills in his apartment were in the name of Isabel Arenas de Martinez—in the Hispanic culture, a married woman adds the surname of her husband to her own name. Police found an American-manufactured ring in the apartment, a ring with the inscription "Ricardo" on the inside, and also recovered a business card suggesting "Ricardo" had worked as a sales representative for a local bookstore chain.

The frenzied local news media jumped on the story and started spewing out additional facts, details—and rumors. One of the major mainstream papers, *Universal*, ran story after story about the "woman who was savagely murdered in the Colonia del Valle." A rival paper, *La Prensa*, fanned the flames of an aroused public by identifying the killer as an *Ex-Combatiente de Vietnam el Asesino*. The killer, said the paper, had been describing himself during his time in Mexico City as a Vietnam War veteran.

It wasn't until the third day after the murder that *La Prensa* ran the first picture of the prime suspect, calling him by the name Ricardo Martinez. The killer was described as 1.70 meters tall—about five feet, six inches—about thirty-two years of age, and sporting straight dark hair and a trimmed mustache.

Inevitably, the weekly magazines that rivaled American tabloids like the *National Enquirer* weighed in with their own accounts. *Alerta* plastered gruesome death scene photos beneath hysterical headlines on its front page, labeling the killer *Cayo el Chacal de Coyoacan*—the Jackal of Coyoacan. The most graphic untouched photo in the front-page spread showed the victim lying facedown on a bloodied, disheveled mattress, her long brown hair falling around her and obscuring the awful injuries to her face and head. The smaller accompanying photo of the suspect showed a man with a receding hairline and a thin mustache, wearing a shirt and tie. *Alerta*'s next edition had a blow-up photo of the killer covering its entire front page; the inside story was headlined *El Sanguinario Maniatico Sexual*—the Bloody Sex Maniac.

The pattern, more brutal than ever, had repeated itself. Ricardo Caputo had loved and then destroyed the object of his love, had run from the scene and disappeared into his familiar invisibility. The cops, still another set on the trail of a beast, found themselves pursuing a ghost.

Ghost, violent beast, invisible man—Ricardo Caputo was certifiably all of those things. It would be eight years before he would again emerge from the shadows, again in connection with a murder. Had the beast within him withdrawn or lost its blood lust for those eight years? Or was it—was he—waiting constantly for fresh victims?

CHAPTER ELEVEN

Now entering his late twenties, Ricardo Caputo had become the ultimate cipher, capable of slithering between cities and groups of acquaintances without ever leaving an indelible mark. He would later say he spent the years after his murder of Laura Gomez mostly in cities in the United States, though his attorney would amend that to claim he'd also traveled back to his native Argentina or Latin America. His restless nature and his fugitive status at once propelled him in his wanderings and prevented him from putting down roots that would seem in any way to be permanent.

Within days of the Gomez murder, with the headlines in Mexico City still screaming for his head and a new manhunt under way, Caputo shot out of Mexico and somehow managed to cross the U.S. border without arousing any suspicions. He would land some two thousand miles to the north, in Salt Lake City, Utah, a Mormon city where strict living and religious codes might have posed a threat to an unprepared stranger who happened also to be a foreigner, and an illegal immigrant at that. But Salt Lake City shared one common trait with New York, Mexico City, and San Francisco—it was a bustling convention center with plenty of hotels and restaurants in constant need of the grunt-work job skills Caputo possessed. Once again he took on a series of jobs as waiter and busboy, though in less than half a year the gaucho within him got his feet moving, west this time to Los Angeles.

If Ricardo was aware that outstanding federal warrants describing him as a dangerous serial murderer might have resulted in his arrest at any time, he didn't show it in the City of Angels. He dove right in, once again successfully aiming his skill at anonymity toward a subsistence life in menial service jobs, but eventually, law enforcement sources say, he landed a job as a restaurant manager, which was a first step up the ladder for him and a precursor to jobs he would later secure and thrive in. The attorney who represented Caputo after his surrender in New York, Michael Kennedy, claimed his client proved to himself in Los Angeles that he could hold down a responsible job, one that was a match for his skills. Detectives who later spoke with Caputo also say that in Los Angeles the four-time killer took up with another woman, whom they identified as Jasmine Fernandez, marrying her in 1979 and signaling what he would later describe in his diaries as a period of relative stability in his life. He did say in those same diaries that the marriage did not get off to an auspicious start because he was "hearing voices." The voices disturbed him, he said, but did not lead to a full-fledged depression. According to an account of his self-described diaries in the *New York Times*, Caputo claimed he even spoke to his wife's mother about the "voices," but that she dismissed them as a result of overwork. Caputo remained in the marriage, and in 1981 his wife bore him a son, followed quickly by a daughter.

It was the day after his daughter was born, Caputo would claim, that he abandoned his family and Los Angeles for good. He said he left because he thought his wife feared that he had been having conversations with people who didn't exist.

During his Los Angeles years, his victims' families and the law enforcement officials who'd been frustrated so thoroughly never fully suspended their attempts to bring the ladykiller to justice.

San Francisco Police Inspector Earl Sanders always had feelers out, and was never far removed from the bulging case file on the man who'd murdered Barbara Taylor in 1975.

"There was always information dribbling in on him," Sanders recalled, "from people who'd met him or from past friends of his we'd always stay in touch with. Everything we got, we shared with the FBI, but Caputo never surfaced. We did know he had a brother in New York . . ."

The details of the connection between Ricardo Caputo and his younger brother, Alberto, have always been a mystery. Certain law enforcement investigators who'd stayed on the killer's trail suspected that Alberto may have been aware of his brother's life on the run. But efforts of law enforcement officials to prove a connection failed.

At the same time, law enforcement sources were reluctant to share all they knew with the families of Ricardo Caputo's victims. Jane Becker, tireless in her search for any morsel of information that might have helped corral her daughter Judy's killer, knew that Ricardo had a brother. She believed Alberto had friends who ran a shop in New York City that Ricardo had frequented when he was being treated on Wards Island. Jane Becker was reduced after a while to writing letters in hopes of keeping the vigilance of law enforcement at an active pitch. When she heard about Caputo's escape from the detention center in El Paso, Texas, and learned in the following weeks about the murder at his hands of Barbara Taylor in San Francisco just prior to the escape, she wrote to Mexican authorities with the idea of warning them: a serial killer, a dangerous man, is probably on his way to Mexico if he isn't already there. She got no response. When she learned years later that Caputo was the suspect in the murder of Laura Gomez, she was driven once again to the depths of despair and frustration. I'd warned them, I'd warned them! she thought. No one ever bothered to respond, she lamented; and now another young woman, another life full of promise, had been taken.

After leaving his wife and children in Los Angeles, Ricardo Caputo claims he traveled back to Mexico once again, this time under the alias Roberto Dominguez. But law enforcement officials believe that at some point he may have snuck in a side trip to the East Coast. He was in dire straits, they guessed, and in need of help. His brother Alberto? they wondered. The tips about Alberto had been run to the ground and had produced nothing, but it was time to take another, perhaps closer look at the older of the two brothers.

"It was always our understanding," recalled San Francisco Police Inspector Earl Sanders, "that Ricardo adored his older brother. That's the word we heard. If you adore someone, you find a way to stay in contact with him. That was the extent of the lead that brought us back to the subject of Alberto."

Beyond their birth origins in Mendoza, Argentina, and the fact that they'd arrived in New York City at roughly the same time, Alberto Caputo was his brother's opposite in nearly every significant way. From their similar humble beginnings in a broken and then restructured home, Ricardo developed a clever way about him and dabbled in drawing and languages, but stumbled at age eighteen into needed treatment for depression in a mental institution in Argentina. Alberto, meanwhile, figured out that the route to the top was a straight line paved by a willingness to work, and work he did.

When he landed his first full-time job in New York, sweeping floors at the Lexington Photographic Labs in midtown, he stayed the course and stayed put, working his way up inexorably in management positions throughout the 1970s until, in 1979, he was named president and chief executive officer.

Lexington Photo Labs is presently located in a commercial-industrial building at 49 West Twenty-third Street in Manhattan. The black polished front facade and the glass and metal doors throw back the reflections of pedestrian passersby, its block of Twenty-third Street one of the busiest in an always bustling neighborhood. Employees of the hundreds of businesses that cram the block are known to race around during the working day, gulping sandwiches or slices of pizza or running errands during their hectic lunch hours or mini-breaks.

Visitors to Lexington Photo take a quick ride up to the fourth floor, where the elevator opens right into the business. The plain entranceway reveals in modest form its obvious success. The white service counter runs the entire width of the room, and features a multiline phone and a plain business-card holder. Beyond the counter a visitor can peruse a collection of high-quality photographs—the lab's work, of course—all of the photos tastefully displayed in flattering light. There's a close-up of a beautiful model's sharply featured face, and richly detailed posters of city scenes in color and black and white. The smell of lab chemicals wafts subtly through the air, evidence, if it was needed, that the lab's twenty-four employees are hard at work.

The business, say law enforcement sources, grosses

millions of dollars a year and has provided Alberto Caputo with a life of comfortable opulence. He was able to put a half million dollars down on a $900,000 home in an exclusive enclave in Riverdale, New York, just north of the city. The home, in the enclave known to its residents as Fieldston, sits in the shadow of Manhattan College and peers out over the scenic Hudson River. Like its neighboring homes, Caputo's residence is nestled in an expanse of manicured lawns and recently pruned shrubs. The white stucco and gray-shingled home is barely visible over a six-foot-high wooden fence, though its two brick chimneys and gabled windows on the second floor are in full view between the embracing branches of tall trees. The house numbers are only displayed on a small vertical sign posted on the fence in front of the driveway. An American flag adorns the Caputos' simple black mailbox.

The privacy of the Caputo residence is enhanced by its location on a dead-end block on the crest of a gently sloping hill. The tony and very private Fieldston School is a short ride away. Motorists who stumble into the neighborhood are given notice that it is not a neighborhood in which to languish. Black and white signs, posted discreetly at the heads of most of the through streets, tell them:

Fieldston:
Speed limit 25 miles per hour
A private community

Private streets
No parking
No soliciting
No commercial traffic
Illegally parked cars will be removed at owner's
expense

The Fieldston Property Owners Association

The more law enforcement authorities studied the
life and lifestyle of Alberto Caputo and his wife, the
former Kimberly Zorn, the more they speculated as
to where Ricardo Caputo could run if his world
started closing in on him.

Alberto, they knew, had accumulated properties
around the state of New York, including several ad-
dresses in Brooklyn and Queens and another resi-
dential dwelling in Pound Ridge, in Westchester
County. They were also intrigued by a seventy-five-
acre spread he'd purchased in Preston Hollow, a pic-
turesque hamlet in the town of Rensselaerville in upstate New York. The guy was loaded, officials
concluded, and also owned methods of transport that
could have entertained dozens of people in style—
Range Rovers and BMWs and Jeeps, a few motorcy-
cles and two swift powerboats.

Despite their suspicions, investigators were hard-
pressed to find evidence exposing direct contact between the brothers.

And if Ricardo Caputo was in New York in the
early to mid-eighties, as authorities believe he was,

though he denies it, then it made sense—and does to this day—to consider his name in conjunction with the murder of still another woman.

Still another unsolved murder, in Manhattan, in the first week of August 1983.

CHAPTER TWELVE

Ricardo Caputo denies it. His lawyer, Michael Kennedy, denies it on his client's behalf. But with Caputo's surrender having re-energized dormant investigations of other long-unsolved homicides, there is renewed belief among law enforcement sources that Caputo may have been responsible for the 1983 murder of Manhattan author-activist Jacqueline Bernard.

Livia Turgeon and Beverly Daniels were the last people to see Jacqueline Bernard alive. August 1 of that summer was a sweltering summer night, and the three women decided to escape the heat by taking in a movie in an air-conditioned theater. They watched a Polish film, *Ways in the Night*, in a movie house on Broadway and Sixty-sixth Street. Then they grabbed some Italian food in an Amsterdam Avenue restaurant, walking a block back to Broadway afterward to board an uptown bus for the ride home. Jacqui, as she liked to be called, was the last of the three to get off the bus.

The next time Livia Turgeon heard anything about

Jacqui was when a friend called her late the next day in her campus office at Columbia University, where she taught a course in the field of biostatistics. What had Livia heard or what did she know, the friend asked her, about Jacqui's death?

Jacqui's death? Livia Turgeon couldn't believe it. Jacqui was known to her family and to her hundreds of friends and acquaintances as a vibrant, insistently alive, healthy, and physically active woman on Manhattan's Upper West Side. She was often seen biking around the city, but those who knew her were most impressed by her political, community, and cultural activism, and by a desire she demonstrated throughout her life to lend her own voice to those who by themselves could not be heard.

Born to a French father and an American mother and raised in the United States, Bernard was sixty-two and had been divorced for a quarter century at the time of her death. She'd filled those years with one project after another, devoting astonishing energy to each task at hand and to her abiding interest in public issues.

As an author, she was much accomplished and respected nationally, having written *Journey Toward Freedom,* an acclaimed biography of the black female abolitionist Sojourner Truth; *Voices from the Southwest,* a book of profiles of enduring figures who, as American Indians or early Spanish settlers, helped define the American Southwest; and *The History You Gave Us,* a chronicle of the early years of the Jewish Child Care Association of New York.

Jacqui Bernard also had a penchant for folding her personal experiences into projects or programs that would benefit others with like experiences. In 1956 she was one of the founders of Parents Without Partners, an organization that went a long way toward removing the stigma endured by divorced and single parents and identifying the common problems with which those parents and their children would likely have to cope. The national membership of Parents Without Partners eventually numbered in the hundreds of thousands.

Jacqui would also turn the tables and allow her activities and pursuits to change her own flexible self-image. In the June before her death, she received her B.A. degree in medical anthropology from the New School for Social Research and immediately left for conferences in her new specialty in New Hampshire and Cuba. The developments reversed behavior from her early years, when she was an indifferent student who'd quit prestigious Vassar College and then the equally prestigious University of Chicago to run off to Mexico and try her hand at journalism. In Mexico she'd met and married a fellow journalist named Allen Bernard, and though the union was a struggle and eventually foundered, it produced a son, Joel, before the couple divorced.

After the divorce, Jacqui Bernard settled in on Manhattan's Upper West Side, the hip and vaguely bohemian edge of New York City that projected a free-form style of living and a variety of cultural, culinary, and political offerings. The changing maze of daily options suited Jacqui's independent needs, and provided limitless energy for a brilliant woman who wanted to learn and experience as much as she could. She frequented the coffeehouses, jazz clubs, and shops that lined Broadway, Columbus, and Amsterdam Avenues, leaving behind a reputation that was only reinforced and reconfirmed as the years went by as a woman who was intelligent, warm, genuinely caring and generous. One investigator who'd pored through her life concluded, "She was the epitome of the literate radical."

Open as she was to the limitless possibilities of life, it was hardly out of character for Jacqui Bernard to organized an impromptu movie date with friends.

But everything about her death, it turned out, was wrong.

On Tuesday evening, August 2, 1986, Jacqui's sister Henriette and Henriette's husband, Robert Montgomery, became concerned when Jacqui failed to show up for dinner. She didn't miss dinners or break appointments unless there was a good reason, and if there was a good reason, she would always call. The couple waited with growing concern, and after calling Jacqui's number several more times and getting no answer, they finally decided to travel to the apart-

A young Ricardo Caputo is taken into custody hours after admitting to the July 31, 1971 murder of Natalie Brown in her Flower Hill, Long Island home. (STAN WOLFSON, *NEWSDAY*)

Natalie Brown, shown in her 1969 yearbook photograph from Roslyn High School. She was described as a fun-loving teenager who excelled at swimming and horseback riding. (COURTESY OF *NEWSDAY*)

Barbara Taylor, a sophisticated film executive, was found stomped to death in the bedroom of her San Francisco apartment. Her body was discovered days after Ricardo Caputo had returned to the apartment from a trip to Hawaii. (BILL YOUNG, *SAN FRANCISCO CHRONICLE*)

Ricardo Caputo in happier times. This photograph was distributed by San Francisco police after the Easter Sunday, 1975 murder of film executive Barbara Taylor.
(SAN FRANCISCO CHRONICLE)

Ricardo Caputo sitting poolside with his second victim, psychologist Judy Becker. This photograph was taken at the Bridgewater, Connecticut home of Becker's parents just months before they found her strangled to death.
(NEW YORK CITY POLICE DEPARTMENT)

RECOMPENSA DE $25,000

Por informacion que faci lite la detencion y condena
del individuo o individuos que mataro a

**JACQUELINE BERNARD
552 RIVERSIDE DRIVE**

la noche del 1 de agosto de 1983.
Una bolsa grande de color gris y de nylon asi como
un relof de pulsera de oro, y plata con grabados
tipo mexicano, fueron robados. Toda informacion
recibida sera de caracter estric tamente confidencial.

**SIMUASE A LLAMAN AL TELEFONO
598-0071
(SERVICIO LAS 24 HORAS)**

This flyer was distributed throughout Manhattan's Upper West Side after Jacqueline Bernard's family posted a $25,000 reward for information about her murder on August 1, 1983. Ricardo Caputo was not considered a suspect at that time.

(JONATHAN GORDON ASSOCIATES)

Two years after Jacqueline Bernard's 1983 murder, private investigators for the family distributed this flyer after an anonymous informant gave information leading police to suspect Ricardo Caputo. Police are still hoping the informant, with code name "J-22 ," will come forward again.

(JONATHAN GORDON ASSOCIATES)

Who Killed Jacqui Bernard?

The man in this photo, Ricardo (Ricky or Richie) Caputo, is a strong suspect in the murder of Jacqueline Bernard on August 2, 1983. He has also used aliases Robert Diaz or Robert Ruiz, as well as other names.

Caputo is also wanted in connection with the murders of two other women. He was born in Argentina and is 32 years old. He is 5'7" or 5'8", 150-160 pounds, and has brown hair and eyes. These photos were taken about 10 years ago, and he may have grown a mustache. His hair may be thinning.

Caputo has worked as a waiter and busboy on the West Side of New York City. He is intelligent and well-spoken. He speaks several languages and is artistic. He may have met Jacqueline Bernard a few months before her death at an outing, party, or trip, or at a bar on the West Side. She may have been helping him with legal problems. He may have borrowed her car on the night of her murder or on other occasions.

If you have any information about Caputo, if you can identify the occasion on which he met Jacqueline Bernard, if you saw them together, or if you can recall any conversation regarding him, please call Gordon McEwan at 212-570-2967. Jonathan Gordon Investigations. All information will be kept strictly confidential.

Please circulate this letter among the friends of Jacqueline Bernard and the organizations with which she was connected.

Jacqueline Bernard's apartment on Manhattan's Riverside Drive was an ongoing project in her life. It is also where her body was found on August 1, 1983. (JULIET PAPA)

The Odell Avenue apartment in Yonkers, New York where the strangled and beaten body of Judy Becker was found by her parents. They feared the worst after not hearing from her following a scheduled weekend boat trip with Ricardo Caputo. (JULIET PAPA)

The Flower Hill, Long Island home of murder victim Natalie Brown. Police discovered her body on the kitchen floor, stabbed repeatedly. Police picked up Ricardo Caputo at a nearby pay phone after he'd called them to report the murder. (JULIET PAPA)

The Cicero, Illinois home where Ricardo Caputo lived under the alias of Franco Porraz. He kept his identity and his past a secret while raising a family and working as a waiter in one of Chicago's most popular restaurants. (Mike Taibbi)

Harry Caray's, a sports bar and restaurant owned by the legendary announcer for the Chicago Cubs baseball team. Ricardo Caputo worked there under the alias Frank Porraz and became one of the restaurant's most popular and productive waiters. Customers asked for him even after he stopped working there. (Mike Taibbi)

Photograph of Ricardo Caputo after his March 9, 1994 surrender. This was taken after his appearance and confession on the national television broadcast of ABC's "Prime Time Live." He portrayed himself as a man driven to murder by periodic bouts of mental illness. (NASSAU COUNTY POLICE)

Officials in Nassau County escort Ricardo Caputo to his first court appearance following his surrender on March 9, 1994. He returned to Long Island to face charges relating to the murder of Natalie Brown, whom he had admitted to killing 23 years earlier. (STEVE BERMAN)

Ricardo Caputo's first appearance in State Supreme Court in Mineola, Long Island after his surrender. He was accompanied by high-powered New York City attorney Michael Kennedy, who plans to pursue an insanity defense.
(DICK YARWOOD, *NEWSDAY*)

ment and check things out for themselves. When they got there, the super let them into Jacqui's fourth floor co-op, apartment 4K, with a spare key. They found her body, prone and face down on her own bed. The couple summoned police from the Twenty-sixth Precinct station house, and a squad car was dispatched for the trip of less than two blocks to Bernard's apartment at 552 Riverside Drive.

The two officers in the patrol car knew they were responding to the report of a dead body, but suspected no more as they pulled up in front of the white stucco pre-war building just past a cross street called Tiemann Place on Riverside. Several small Columbia University dorms were on the block, they knew. Number 552 Riverside featured an elaborate facade with generous stone trim around a nondescript glass front door. The officers passed through the modest black-and-white-tiled lobby and took the elevator up to the fourth floor.

Once inside number 4K, they were led by the victim's sister and brother-in-law through the apartment and into the bedroom. They looked around quickly, expertly, but saw nothing out of the ordinary or, apparently, out of place. Jacqui Bernard was clothed in a polyester robe, and the outfit she'd worn the night before was neatly folded and set aside. The cops, having called for a unit from the precinct Detective Squad, saw nothing in their silent perusal to suggest a break-in, a robbery, or a struggle between the deceased and anyone else.

The detectives who quickly arrived seemed to agree, working on the initial premise that Jacqui Bernard had died of natural causes. But her sister and brother-in-law, along with her son Joel, insisted that a medical examiner should conduct an autopsy, standard practice whenever there are possibly mysterious circumstances surrounding a death. She'd been so healthy and alive, her family insisted. The friends who'd attended the movie with her the night before concurred; there'd been no hint anything was wrong. A neighbor said Jacqui had recently been sawing wood for some fix-up in her apartment before her death.

An autopsy was ordered, and conducted the next day by then Chief Medical Examiner Elliot Gross; the finding was a shocker. Jacqueline Bernard's larynx had been fractured; she had been strangled to death! One detective later said, "This wasn't a ligature strangulation, it was simple force." He summoned a cop term. "She was yoked. Her neck was in the crook of someone's arm, someone strong. And that someone just pulled."

Jacqui Bernard's family was incensed. Since the police officers and detectives who'd responded originally judged the death to be the result of natural causes, and not a homicide or even a possible homicide, the apartment had not been treated like a crime scene. The standard analyses and checks on everything from fingerprints to hair samples to blood and skin residue were not conducted that night, and now the "crime scene" had been trampled, disturbed, and in other ways "infected."

The family decided swiftly to take action on their own, led by Jacqui's brother-in-law Robert Montgomery, a successful attorney and partner with the top-shelf Manhattan firm of Paul, Weiss, Rifkind, Wharton and Garrison. Montgomery networked and put out the word that he was looking to hire a team of top private investigators to make up the ground lost by the New York City Police Department. In short order Montgomery retained the services of Jonathan Gordon Investigations, which had been recommended to Montgomery by the famous and controversial attorney Roy Cohn. The two partners who'd formed Jonathan Gordon Investigations, John McGrath and Gordon McEwan, had already done considerable work for Cohn and had evidently impressed him enough to move to the top of his list of private eye referrals.

McGrath and McEwan, both retired New York City police detectives, had started as partners straight out of the Police Academy, and each, over the years, had collected a laundry list of commendations and investigative credits. They'd begun their careers in 1963 by being assigned to the newly formed Tactical Patrol Unit, which patrolled the civil rights riots of the decade. Later in their careers, after making detective grade, they were transferred together to the Safe,

Loft and Truck Unit, which investigated high-brow and high-profile theft operations. The pair split up briefly when McGrath went over to Brooklyn Homicide and pioneered the command's hypnosis unit. Both men retired, putting in their papers together, in 1982, and immediately joined forces again, only this time in the private sector. They were a formidable team by then; McGrath stood six-three, with a thick shock of blond hair and twinkly blue eyes he used to mask an instinct for the jugular and his keen perceptive skills; McEwan, only an inch shorter, probed his subjects with deep brown eyes and a quiet, stubborn intelligence.

When Robert Montgomery hired the two private eyes, they got down to work immediately and came up with some quick findings suggesting that whoever murdered Jacqui Bernard was likely someone she knew.

"We came up with traces of human feces," McGrath said. "Once you're choked, your bowels let go. We were pretty sure whoever did it was someone who was let into the apartment. Why would an intruder go through the machinations of cleaning up the victim and then changing her into her nightgown? An intruder wouldn't go through the effort of covering it up, and a simple burglar wouldn't have cared one way or the other."

Two days after her death, Jacqui's pocketbook, minus any cash, turned up in a Bronx post office. Someone had dropped it in a mailbox, but it was never made clear whether the purse had been taken from her apartment the night of her death or whether she'd left it on the uptown bus coming home from the movies and dinner earlier in the evening. McGrath and McEwan pressed forward on the robbery angle, their own interviews leading them to conclude that some etchings and a Mexican-made watch were also missing from the apartment.

The cops weren't making as much progress as the two private eyes were, so they took the case to the streets. Jacqui's son Joel said he'd post a reward, and the investigators used that offer to top what they hoped would be a massive publicity campaign designed to drum up tips from a neighborhood where the victim was so well-known. They enlisted many of Jacqui's friends to distribute posters and leaflets in both English and Spanish; the flyers ended up being plastered on nearly every telephone post, light pole, storefront, parking meter, and mailbox in the neighborhood, each flyer featuring a good-quality photograph of a smiling Jacqui Bernard and the following message:

$25,000 REWARD
FOR INFORMATION LEADING TO THE ARREST AND CONVIC-
TION OF THE PERSON OR PERSONS WHO MURDERED
JACQUELINE BERNARD
552 RIVERSIDE DRIVE
ON THE NIGHT OF AUGUST 1, 1983.

A LARGE GRAY NYLON HANDBAG AND A WATCH WITH AN
ENGRAVED GOLD AND SILVER BAND WITH MEXICAN FIG-
URES WERE TAKEN

ALL REPLIES CONFIDENTIAL
CALL 598-0071
24 HOURS

As the two detectives waited for the calls to come,
and maybe even some real clues worth pouncing on
immediately, they delved into Jacqui Bernard's past,
trying to understand her character and the way she
thought. It was important, in the absence of any hot
leads, to figure out how and why she'd been drawn
into the relationships and friendships in her crowded
life. Busy as she'd always been, the two experienced
detectives knew there was a lot of ground to cover
but that the backward search might help them locate
the markers or personal standards in anyone's life
that could explain a later momentous life event—or a
death.

As the investigators pored over the life of the murdered author, they took particular note of a recent
period in her life when she was apparently drawn to
the issue of prisoners' rights. She helped drum up
attention for a previously little-known book called
The Pretrial Detainees Manual, and on another occasion at about the same time, took it upon herself to
post bail for a teenage defendant in a murder case in
Connecticut. He was wrongfully accused of killing his
mother.

It was helpful, but it didn't get the gumshoes any closer to the man who had fractured Jacqui Bernard's larynx by "yoking" her to death. Other investigations filled out their growing caseload, and finally, more than a year had passed without any significant breakthroughs on the Bernard killing.

Then, on a dreary winter day, one of Gordon McEwan's hot lines started to ring.

CHAPTER THIRTEEN

In the Twenty-sixth Precinct Detective Squad Room records office, the Jacqueline Bernard case occupied two fat brown accordion envelopes. They were wrapped with rubber bands and stashed in a metal file cabinet, occupying a rear portion of the middle drawer. They'd been untouched for months, collecting dust.

"Dust them off," Gordon McEwan said when he called the Detective Squad at the Two-six on January 22, 1985. "I'll be over later this morning."

The call came in that morning as McEwan sipped his coffee in his fourth-floor office suite at 52 Broadway in lower Manhattan. He was doing a mental scan of several ongoing cases, and a look out the window into the parking lot below wasn't the least bit distracting, or inspiring. But when the hot line rang, McEwan stiffened. The line was specified for informants on a variety of cases. When this number lit up, it was usually an important call, but due to the unpredictability of a tipster's motives or desire, no investigator could be sure of how important the call might be. But it was never a call not worth taking. McEwan picked up the phone, and a man's voice was on the other line. As McEwan listened, he waved frantically for McGrath to come into his office. He kept pointing to the phone and mouthing the words "Jacqueline Bernard." As he continued to listen, he wrote the word "informant" on a piece of paper. McGrath didn't dare pick up the extension, for fear of scaring the caller off with the all-too-obvious click. When the call was over, McEwan nearly jumped out of his chair.

"First thing we've got to do," McEwan said to McGrath after the caller hung up, "is reach the Montgomerys!" He was referring, of course, to Jacqui's sister Henriette and her husband Robert, who still had the private eye on retainer. "We have to tell him that someone has given us the name of a guy who bragged about doing Jacqui Bernard's murder!"

John McGrath won't get specific about the call today because some of the information provided by the caller was so detailed that disseminating it publicly before the murder is solved would eliminate its use in tripping up or confirming the stories of anybody who might yet come forward.

"But the caller used the name 'Ricky,'" McGrath says, "and also provided a last name and an alias the killer had used in the past. He said 'Ricky' was very specific about intimate details of the crime," and that the caller, after his conversation with "Ricky," knew an awful lot about the subject.

The two investigators reviewed the homicide file

on Jacqui Bernard's killing and quickly tapped into the network of police department sources they'd maintained since leaving the job. They quickly came up with the name of Ricardo Caputo, his outstanding fugitive and murder warrants jumping out at them. Details from the files about Caputo's life and modus operandi seemed to match some of what their anonymous caller had said about the "confessed" killer of Jacqui Bernard.

With the support of the Montgomerys and the renewed interest of NYPD homicide investigators, the private detectives put together a new flyer, one which, was topped this time by a photograph of Ricardo Caputo. It was a twelve-year-old shot, not the best for their purpose, but it would have to do. And maybe it would do the trick, since their mystery tipster said his own call was prompted by the original poster about the Bernard murder that had been papered around the neighborhood so many long months ago. The investigators had no choice: they had to work with what they had. At least, now, they had a name.

The new poster read this way:

THE MAN IN THIS PHOTO, RICARDO (RICKY OR RICHIE) CAPUTO, IS A STRONG SUSPECT IN THE MURDER OF JACQUELINE BERNARD ON AUGUST 2, 1983. HE HAS ALSO USED THE ALIASES ROBERT DIAZ OR ROBERT RUIZ, AS WELL AS OTHER NAMES.

CAPUTO IS ALSO WANTED IN CONNECTION WITH THE MURDERS OF TWO OTHER WOMEN. HE WAS BORN IN ARGENTINA AND IS 32 YEARS OLD. HE IS 5'7" OR 5'8" AND 150—160 POUNDS, AND HAS BROWN HAIR AND EYES. THESE PHOTOS WERE TAKEN ABOUT TEN YEARS AGO AND HE MAY HAVE GROWN A MUSTACHE. HIS HAIR MAY BE THINNING.

CAPUTO HAS WORKED AS A WAITER AND BUSBOY ON THE WEST SIDE OF NEW YORK CITY. HE IS INTELLIGENT AND WELL-SPOKEN. HE SPEAKS SEVERAL LANGUAGES AND IS ARTISTIC. HE MAY HAVE MET JACQUELINE BERNARD A FEW MONTHS BEFORE HER DEATH AT AN OUTING, PARTY, OR TRIP, OR AT A BAR ON THE WEST SIDE. SHE MAY HAVE BEEN HELPING HIM WITH LEGAL PROBLEMS. HE MAY HAVE BORROWED HER CAR ON THE NIGHT OF HER MURDER OR ON OTHER OCCASIONS.

IF YOU HAVE ANY INFORMATION ABOUT CAPUTO, IF YOU CAN IDENTIFY THE OCCASION ON WHICH HE MET JACQUELINE BERNARD, IF YOU SAW THEM TOGETHER, OR IF YOU CAN RECALL ANY CONVERSATION REGARDING HIM, PLEASE CALL GORDON MCEWAN AT 212-570-2967, JONATHAN GORDON INVESTIGATIONS. ALL INFORMATION WILL BE KEPT STRICTLY CONFIDENTIAL.

PLEASE CIRCULATE THIS LETTER AMONG THE FRIENDS OF JACQUELINE BERNARD AND THE ORGANIZATIONS WITH WHICH SHE WAS CONNECTED.

The posters went up in the usual places, but were also displayed in local bars and restaurants. These were all likely venues for Caputo, who in the past had worked in and patronized trendy eateries and socialized at popular nightspots.

Authorities began following up the fresh lead McEwan gleaned from the male tipster that Jacqui Bernard had befriended a young man in the months before she died. It wasn't a romantic relationship, the tipster said, but rather one in which the man had claimed to need assistance with legal or visa problems; and Jacqui, sympathetic, had said she'd try to help. The tipster had told McEwan that the man and Bernard were seen together in a popular West Side bar, though he wasn't sure which one.

The investigators, along with the cops from Homicide, began canvassing the nightspots that were especially popular on the West Side, at one point looking closely at a veritable institution called the West End Gate. The West End Gate was a hot jazz emporium at 2911 Broadway—still its location—whose laid-back setting, dark smoky bar, and performance stage provided a great social and musical outlet for the neighborhood, as well as drawing visitors from far and wide.

In its past the "Gate" had attracted headliner talent ranging from Dizzy Gillespie to the "Countsmen", who were Count Basie's alumni, and the remaining associates of the late great Charlie Parker. Phil Schaap, who produced and emceed shows at the Gate for twenty-one years, currently broadcasts on Columbia University's radio station WKCR and is considered a knowledgeable historian of Manhattan's West Side. But he couldn't help investigators run down their lead on Jacqui Bernard and her young "friend."

"I knew the whole cast of characters, not only the ones who performed, but the ones who came to watch," Schaap recalled. "Allen Ginsberg used to show up, and so did the Rolling Stones drummer, Charlie Watts. I was here every day for more than twenty years."

But he didn't remember Jacqueline Bernard, a fixture on the West Side.

Gordon McEwan kept hoping the geyser of fresh publicity might convince his original mystery tipster to call again. They gave him the code name "J-22," because he first called January 22. But he never did call again.

McEwan died shortly thereafter, never knowing how or if a case that had bedeviled him would be resolved. For his partner, John McGrath, the Bernard murder remained an active case, and when there was a hopeful lead, he'd check it out. But those were few and far between as Ricardo Caputo remained a fugitive.

Now, with Caputo having surrendered, the New York City Police Department is once again appealing to the public for help. Anyone with any information on the death of Jacqueline Bernard is asked to call the police either at their own hot-line number, 212-577-TIPS, or the detective squad at the Twenty-sixth Precinct, 212-678-1351.

The New York City cop who now heads the Bernard murder investigation is veteran detective Gerry Giorgio. It's the latest in his thick portfolio of high-publicity investigations, his past cases including the "Murder at the Met" homicide, in which a stagehand at the Metropolitan Opera House was charged in the murder of acclaimed violinist Helen Hagnes Mintiks. Giorgio is also currently involved in an active case of a particularly gruesome death, that of a young girl the tabloids dubbed "Baby Hope." The victim's decomposed remains were found in a cooler tossed into the woods off the Henry Hudson Parkway, and the identity of the young victim remains a mystery.

Now Giorgio is steeping himself in the death of Jacqueline Bernard twelve years ago, and in the character and history of Ricardo Caputo, still listed as the "prime suspect" in her murder. "I'd like to talk to him," the detective says of Caputo. "If he wasn't here in New York at the time of the murder, he should have no problem explaining to me exactly where he was."

Caputo says he didn't do it, and his attorney vigorously denies that his client had any involvement in or knowledge of the strangulation killing of Jacqui Bernard. The confessed killer says he was in Mexico at the time, where he'd met another woman. And where he had again fallen in love.

CHAPTER FOURTEEN

Ricardo Caputo may claim he was in Mexico *around* the time of Jacqueline Bernard's murder, but at present it's impossible to determine when exactly he entered and left the country where he'd carried out the "Jackal of Coyoacan" beating death of twenty-year-old Laura Gomez. Confusion over Caputo's precise whereabouts at many points during his years on the run may be due in part to his convenient desire to forget; or because he genuinely may have lost track of the routes and times of his meanderings.

For example, one detective who spoke to the killer after he'd surrendered says Caputo told him he left Los Angeles—with a wife and two children in that city—and, without bothering to obtain a divorce, headed straight for Chicago, where under still another alias he married an American-born Latina woman. Caputo's present attorney disputes this account, insisting that his client returned to South America, where he married his last wife.

But the latest and perhaps most accurate account was given by Caputo himself when he taped the ABC program "Prime Time Live" on March 9, 1994.

Caputo said that after leaving Los Angeles abruptly, he traveled to Guadalajara, about 350 miles to the northwest of Mexico City. Caputo says he took a job there as an English teacher and that it was in that role that he met his current wife. Like Laura Gomez, Susana Alessandra was a student; But Susana, at seventeen, was only half Caputo's age and, unlike Laura, was one of Caputo's own students. The couple married after Caputo agreed to be baptized, and "Prime Time" showed photos of the baptismal ceremony in which Caputo bent his head over the baptismal font while Susana, wearing a smart dark green dress, looked on solemnly.

During this period, Caputo told "Prime Time," he heard no "voices" and felt no violent urges. Asked by correspondent Chris Wallace to explain how he was able to keep himself from killing again, Caputo responded, "Well, I think the love of my wife did it, and the love of my family."

Caputo pulled up stakes in Mexico in 1986 and took his wife to Chicago, where the official records show he embarked on a life of apparent if uncharacteristic, stability. He seemed willing to put down roots as he and Susana began a family, and he sought again to make his mark by using his skills and charm. This time, though, they combined to produce positive, not violent, results, and he quickly became one of the best and most in-demand waiters in the Windy City.

Caputo had hit the most popular places in town

when he first went looking for work, and soon enough found himself being hired as a waiter and eventually a manager at several of the better eateries in town.

Caputo, of course, was not Ricardo Caputo in his Chicago years, but "Franco Porraz." He claimed Mexican and Sicilian heritage, a story he told consistently.

With regular and lucrative employment becoming his welcome habit, "Franco Porraz"—he was also known as Frank—moved his family to Cicero, Illinois, a town of some sixty thousand residents less than a half hour southwest of the Chicago city limits. Perhaps it was only a coincidence—but local mythology has it that another fugitive used Cicero as an effective hideout from the law. That fugitive was Chicago's most infamous gangster, Al Capone, whose reign of terror ignited the 1930s.

What is ironic, and not in dispute, is that "Frank Porraz" actually bought and lived for five years in a home that looked directly across the street at the rear door of the Cicero police station. A records check at that station house shows that neither "Frank Porraz" nor Ricardo Caputo had ever compiled any violations, "not even a traffic ticket," said the sergeant who ran the names on his computer.

The Latino neighborhood Caputo chose was one where he and his Mexican-born wife were most likely to feel comfortable. When he drove to work or when Susana shopped, they would most often travel along

Cicero Avenue, the town's main commercial strip, lined on both sides by carnicerias (butchers), taquerias, cafés, and burrito stands. It was a colorful stretch where logos of flowers and fruit were displayed over Mama Lucy's Botanica, where the huge aquamarine blue and orange sign for the Acapulco Driving School draped the storefront doorway, and a bright neon sign invited nights of dining and dancing at Viva Musica.

Still, despite its festive trappings, Cicero was a town of working-class neighborhoods, in which small homes sat on postage-stamp plots, and where the outreaches of urban decay were visible everywhere around the town's industrial edges.

But Ricardo Caputo seemed eager and happy to settle in. His home at 4920 West Twenty-fifth Street was similar in size and structure to others along the block. It was a cottage-like place with a small patch of backyard and a garage, a one-story residence adorned with modest shrubs and a patch of dandelion-dotted front lawn. Indoor-outdoor carpeting lined the eight steps leading to the screened-in front door, and the red and white wrought-iron handrails were painted carefully to match the awning over the front picture window.

The front door opened immediately into the living room, where the family would relax on two love seats, watching television or serving guests from a bar set against the right-hand wall.

Pink and gray floral tiles covered the living area

floor. The dining room and kitchen were straight ahead, and beyond them, through a small foyer, were the three bedrooms situated in the rear of the house.

Neighbors say that the place was always neat and clean and, despite inexpensive furniture, always seemed to be bright and cheery.

Thirteen-year-old Rosa Leon was there often, babysitting for "Frank" and Susie's three children at the time; Ricky, Bobby, and the daughter who was also known as Susie. Rosa occasionally looked after the family dog called Baker, which "Frank" described as a Chinese Huskie.

Rosa, a pretty young girl with dark brown hair, fingered the necklace that held her name on a chain of Florentine gold as she spoke. Her family had moved to the neighborhood six years ago and lived two doors away from the "Porraz" family. Their own home was more formal than their neighbors', the walls painted pale pink to match the tufted plastic-covered Italianate couch and chairs. An end table with a crystal lamp graced one corner of the living room, and across the room stood an elaborate oak dining room set with matching credenza.

Rosa says her family socialized with the Caputos—the "Porrazs"—as any friendly neighbors might.

"They came over for barbecues or we'd talk on the street," Rosa recalls. "They stayed home a lot." She said Susie—"Frank's" wife—"went to school to study English, and once in a while she cut hair. She cut mine and did a good job."

Rosa then translated for her father, Pedro, who said "Frank" talked to him often, about jobs and work but not much else. "He was always saying he was half Italian and half Mexican," Pedro remembered. "He did tell us at one point they were moving to Mexico; then, after he'd gone out and bought some expensive furniture, Frank came to give his tools away. I thought that was a little strange . . ."

Pedro said "Frank" fought a lot with his son Bobby, "telling him how to do things. But he was good to his wife. She was the one who drove the kids to school every day."

But just two years later, when "Frank Porraz" turned up as Ricardo Caputo on "Prime Time" long after he'd moved from Chicago with little fanfare, his old Cicero block was in an uproar.

Rosa recalls, "I was thinking, 'him'? He was a very nice person. I don't know how he could have done something like that." Her father Pedro added, "I really didn't recognize him. He had a different name. Then, I was scared, remembering that Susie would take our kids to school, and how close we lived . . ."

But if in his Chicago years Ricardo Caputo preferred to talk most about his work, it was with good reason. His wealth of experience in the restaurant business finally landed him a plum job at the renowned Harry Caray's restaurant at 33 West Kinzie Street, in the heart of downtown Chicago. Harry Caray is the legendary play-by-play announcer for the Chicago Cubs, a fixture in the City of Broad Shoulders whose firing, if Cub management ever attempted such a thing, would trigger a fan revolt. For decades a treasured segment of baseball lore in one of the great baseball towns in the world was the sight of old Harry leaning out of his announcer's booth at the ivy-walled sanctum known as Wrigley Field, waving his arms expansively and leading the inevitable packed house in an enthusiastic rendition of "Take Me Out to the Ballgame."

His eatery is a monument befitting his legend, a three-story building in imposing brick and granite, with carved designs framing the windows, gables, and main entrance. The facade is adorned with flags, bunting, and a six-foot-long banner proclaiming Harry's trademark exclamation, "Holy Cow!" With its lively and casual atmosphere and its trappings of local history and tradition, Harry's has long been a hot spot for tourists and locals alike. Customers don't have the luxury of reservations, but the constant crowd suggests that no one seems to mind.

The restaurant features seafood, good thick steaks, and a smattering of Italian dishes, all presented in an atmosphere laden with sports memorabilia. Framed pictures of sportscasters and athletes line the walls, and the black-and-white-tiled floors lead to the stool-ringed bar that looks a block long. It's there where customers can sip an ice cold Bud—which Harry hawks with every second breath—and take in the ambience as well. The bar is the centerpiece of a room that is turn-of-the-century gracious, with slowly circulating ceiling fans and smoked-glass lamps.

But it seems Harry saves the best for last. When his customers leave and look back at the establishment, they see a face they'd be hard-pressed to ever forget: It's Harry, of course, a giant replica of his happy, jowly countenance painted over the width and length of one wall of the three-story building. Thirty feet of Harry's mug, smiling out over Chicago, above the slogan "This Bud's for *You!*"

That's where the man who called himself Franco Porraz worked, and apparently thrived. "Where's Franco?" the regular customers got in the habit of asking, when he wasn't immediately in sight. They had fun with him, they joked around with him. And they spent more money in the joint whenever it was Franco who was serving them.

A fellow waiter, Steve, said "Frank Porraz had the number-one job. He was a great waiter, and an incredible salesman. You'd come in for a twenty-dollar meal and end up happily paying a $120 check when you left. He'd win the dessert contests every time. If a table ordered ten, he'd end up selling them twenty. His ability to persuade was tremendous."

Steve and "Frank" became fast friends. They respected each other's work ethic and often shared a beer after a long night's labor. And, it seemed to Steve at the time, they confided in each other. Steve never knew that many of his friend's stories were pure fiction, though some seemed a little farfetched.

"He told me he spent two years in Hawaii," Steve recalls, "and that he was Mexican and Sicilian. He also said he had served in the Marines on secret missions in Latin and South America." Steve paused. "Looking back, some things didn't add up."

But in the late eighties and early nineties, the two socialized frequently and often helped each other with chores and problems. Steve hosted a surprise birthday party for Frank's wife. "They'd come here Sundays a lot," Steve says. "He told me he met his wife in Guadalajara, that she won a beauty contest. She was taking English classes there and continued once they moved here." Steve says it was clear "Frank" adored his wife.

"His family was number one. For the first time, he told me, he said he was in a 'longer' relationship. He said his wife was a harbor of peace he never had. He was devoted to her."

Steve lives in Park Ridge, an upper-middle-class bedroom community about twenty minutes northwest of Cicero. The divorced father lives alone with his dog, likes to play his music at impressive volume on a state-of-the-art stereo system, and drives a late-model pickup truck. As he talked about "Frank," he was cooking up some sausages for a late lunch before heading over to Harry's for the Saturday night shift, the busiest of the week.

"Frank often came over and sat with me here in the kitchen," Steve remembered, extending an arm to draw attention to the sparkling brick-tiled floor and smoothly reconditioned wooden kitchen cabinets. "Frank helped me repair those cabinets," he said. "He had two good hands, he could fix anything. He was generous too; he'd go out of his way for you."

Steve did recall there were times "Frank" got angry. "He was kind of aggressive, I guess. If people got in his way, he'd become aggressive. But at the same time," he hastened to add, "people loved him. Customers, other employees. The waitresses at the restaurant would line up at work for one of his back rubs."

Steve said at first that "Frank" quit Harry Caray's, but quickly amended that account. Actually, he said without elaborating, there was some sort of problem with a customer. The last Steve knew, "Frank" had landed a job as a waiter at the restaurant at Arlington Raceway, a former manager at Harry's greasing the way.

"Sometimes we talked about our personal lives," Steve said of the years when he knew "Frank," though his friend stopped short of ever getting into too much detail. "I remember a few things, that he said he had a poor childhood, had suffered a lot of downs, and that he used to work on ships as a cleaner. We did talk about death a lot, but it was always more of a philosophical discussion. I mean I remember telling him that my parents had survived the war, but that for a long time I went to Auschwitz

every year to leave flowers there." Steve couldn't recall a single specific thing "Frank" had offered him
on the subject of death, and then shook his head
when the discussion turned to Frank's real identity—
and real history.

"I wasn't shocked, but I was surely surprised when
I picked up the paper that morning," Steve recalled,
"and read that Frank Porraz and Ricardo Caputo
were one and the same. An admitted killer! My
daughter's fourteen, she knew him, and she says she
never felt fear or danger with him."

Steve clung tenaciously to the view he preferred of
a man he'd considered a genuine friend.

"I like him so much, he was so good to me and my
family. Now that he's come forward and surrendered? I don't know, if I had young kids and I was
his age, I would not have come forward. But if you
look at it in black and white, he did the right thing. If
he was feeling those urges and temptations, then he
did right for his family."

Steve let his thoughts drift and looked at his
kitchen wall clock. It was time to get to work.

"You know, some people still come in and ask for
him. Ask for Frank. He was the biggest charmer in
the world. Ricardo Caputo I don't know, never did.
Frank Porraz was a great friend. And a great person."

But for "Frank Porraz" of Cicero, Illinois, the se-
renity of what appeared to those who knew him to be
an all-American life was about to be shattered by talk

of death and inhuman savagery. The blasting cap for the explosion was the television show that would splash the murderous past of Ricardo Caputo across the American landscape.

CHAPTER FIFTEEN

On the night of July 28, 1991, millions of Americans sat down in front of their television sets to watch that week's edition of Fox Television's popular program "America's Most Wanted." Every week since its inception three years earlier, the show had devoted its segments to the cases of violent and dangerous fugitives wanted by law enforcement agencies around the country.

But this broadcast was going to be different. For the first time in its history the show was going to profile just one case. Based on a review of available subjects—and at the urging of the Federal Bureau of Investigation, which had become a participant in many shows—the producers selected a murder suspect whom host John Walsh called "the most wanted man in America." That man was Ricardo Caputo.

Sinister music accompanied the opening collage of violence dramatized on the screen. The scenes showed one man exploding in bursts of unspeakable rage—a rage that again and again ended in murder.

Narrator: "He's charming, seductive, deadly. Police say he's a predator who stalks young women. A

serial killer who will kill again. Tonight, you can help stop him. He's a ladykiller—the most wanted man in America."

On the screen, host John Walsh emerged out of the darkness wearing a black suit, red tie, and white handkerchief in his breast pocket. He peered into the lens and spoke directly to his audience.

"The portrait of a serial killer is always a chilling one, shrouded in questions, hidden in shadows. Good evening, I'm John Walsh. Imagine how terrifying it would be to learn that someone you know—your neighbor, your boyfriend—had a dark secret: the urge to kill. Police say Ricardo Caputo is a serial killer, a predator wearing the mask of a completely normal man. Exactly twenty years ago tonight, Natalie Brown was dating Ricardo Caputo. She was living at home with her parents in Roslyn, New York, and she thought she knew her boyfriend pretty well.

"Actually, she didn't know him at all. He's a ladykiller, and tonight he's the most wanted man in America."

That last theme having been pounded home, the show then reprised the four known murders and the El Paso escape through the device of graphic dramatizations. The narration also called Caputo a "prime suspect" in Jacqueline Bernard's murder in 1983.

At the end of the segment, the show broadcast a hot-line number for anyone with information on the case. By the time the credits were scrolling up the screen, the phones were ringing off the hook.

"I think we got a total of 475 tips on the first night the show aired," recalls producer Peter Sparrow, "and out of that we got 153 legitimate leads. Obviously it takes a while to sort through all that, and unfortunately, none of the leads were the type you'd roll on immediately."

While the show was on the air, FBI agents were assigned to sit in the studio and stand ready to respond to any call that seemed like a legitimate tip. There was one call, Sparrow says, that was as promising as it was frustrating.

"We got a tip placing Caputo in Illinois in the neighborhood where, it turned out, he was actually living. A guy said he'd been working on his car in front of his house about a block from where Caputo lived, though he didn't know that. He said Caputo came over to him to talk about the car. They had a conversation. The caller said this happened the day before he saw the show, but he emphasized he didn't know where the guy lived; he'd just met him on the street. It wasn't enough to follow up on. The things we look for when we review tips are either that several people are giving us the same information, or that the caller *knew* the guy had committed those crimes, or—the classic—he was standing behind me in line a few minutes ago!"

Sparrow says that never happened in the Caputo case, although each time the show aired, the studio phone banks were swamped with calls. The response was a testament to two truths that are clear as daylight, in hindsight: Caputo had traveled all over the map, and he was never quite as "invisible" as he'd come to believe he was.

In the week after the show ran, an additional five hundred calls poured in. "And when we ran the show a second time, on September fourteenth," Sparrow recalls, "Caputo was apparently still living in the Chicago area. People called in and said they saw him at a bar, or they worked with him; then there were other calls from all over the country. Still, though, there was nothing specific enough to jump out at us and say, 'Get moving!' "

Special Agent Rick Smith is a spokesman for the FBI's San Francisco office, which had been drawn into the Caputo case after his escape from El Paso following Barbara Taylor's murder. Smith was a big supporter of the television dramatization that had so rekindled public interest in and response to cases that had stymied law enforcement.

"The people at 'America's Most Wanted,' " Smith says, "assisted in keeping the case alive, and in keeping the public interested. None of the shows may have led to an arrest, but they were valuable to us nonetheless. In all, including the tips we [the FBI] got directly, the shows generated some fifteen hundred leads, and we ended up pursuing around twelve hundred of them." Smith paused in his recollection. "It's just that none of the leads led to his capture . . ."

Why was Ricardo Caputo singled out for unprecedented treatment by the show? He never actually had been named on the FBI's "Most Wanted" list. Yet it was agreed by both the bureau and the show's producers, that the Caputo case was one in which massive media exposure could help greatly. Such exposure had been discussed several years earlier, but the producers at the time concluded the story was too complex and inaccessible to put together effectively. They changed their minds only after the decision was made to devote an entire show to tell one story, an unfinished story that might include still more victims.

"I know some consider this a 'fugitive chaser' show," says managing editor Phil Lerman, "but we consider it to be a victims' advocate show. Many of the families in this case have been waiting a long time —a very long time—for justice. In this case there was also the reasonable fear that since Caputo had committed these terrible crimes, he was certainly capable of committing more."

Producer Sparrow added, "This is one of only a few examples we've come across of a known serial killer with a very clear modus operandi. Most serial killers remain unknown for years, if they're ever known. Police tie the series of their crimes through evidence, and often never learn who the killer is. But this case is the exact opposite. They've known who he is since the first crime and now can tie him to four brutal murders of young women he was romantically involved with. We felt that because of his known pat-

terns of behavior and his demonstrated ability to in-
gratiate himself with women, he was likely to be
continuing to commit similar murders. He was probably going to be difficult if not impossible to catch
without national media exposure."

Sparrow is convinced that the show flushed Caputo
out of Chicago. "I hear he denies having seen the
show, but I don't believe that." And surely, Sparrow
said, the ratings—and the response the show got
from callers in the Chicago area—guaranteed it had
been talked about, talk that certainly would have
reached the ears of the very public restaurant manager who went by the name Franco Porraz.

If Sparrow's suspicions are accurate, then Caputo,
as "Franco Porraz" in Chicago, undoubtedly felt the
walls closing in on him, a desperate man compelled
once again to hit the road. He changed jobs, laid low,
and within months put his Cicero home up for sale.
By the spring he had a buyer, the Nonato family, and
he was more than accommodating with them.

Reyes Nonato recalls, "I thought he was a real
friendly person. He talked in a nice manner, and
whenever we came by, before the sale, he always
made me feel at home." She was also impressed by
the concern and thoughtfulness "Frank" showed
over a potential problem concerning new tenants to
whom he'd already offered to rent his basement
apartment.

"We hadn't signed the papers yet," Reyes remembered, "and he called to say he'd planned to rent the

basement to another couple before he'd put the house up for sale. He said he was so sure we were going to get the house that he felt he should call and ask us about the new tenants, to know if we would be satisfied if they did rent the basement."

By June, Reyes and José Nonato and their young son had moved in, not having been aware of the "America's Most Wanted" show and thus having no clue as to who their seller, "Frank Porraz," really was. In fact the two families had become friendly and had even socialized on occasion before the Porrazs left town.

José Nonato remembers "Frank" explaining how his wife Susie was returning to Mexico but that he was going to take a job in a state down south, Kentucky or Tennessee, he recalled. "I knew it was none of my business," Reyes said, "but I thought they were separating and that that's why they were selling."

Just before Susie Porraz was scheduled to leave the country for Mexico, the new owners of the home at 4920 West Twenty-fifth Street in Cicero invited the old owners for a holiday barbecue—Fourth of July. "We spent a nice afternoon with them," Reyes Nonato said. "Then she left, but he still stayed around for a couple of weeks. He'd call and come by for the mail and sometimes sit and talk with us. He even rented our garage for his dog, for a while, because he said he hadn't decided whether the dog was going to go with him. He'd come and clean the garage, and take the dog for a walk."

"All in all," she recalled, "everything went smoothly with the Porraz family. He seemed like he was responsible for his family. He seemed to know his business."

But three years later Reyes Nonato watched with growing horror as another television program depicted "Frank," the mild-mannered man who'd sold her family their new home, as a heartless—and possibly insane—multiple killer.

CHAPTER SIXTEEN

By his own claim, Ricardo Caputo joined his wife Susana and their children in Mexico after leaving Chicago. There never was any job waiting for him "down south in Kentucky or Tennessee." But there was something that was threatening the relative stability, peace, and security that seemed to have permeated his life during his years in Chicago with his family. It was an all-too-familiar undercurrent, an emotional shift that, like an earthquake, began rumbling beneath the surface of Caputo's outward calm. What triggered it remains a mystery; perhaps as in the past, when he left his wife in California after his daughter was born, the birth of his fourth child with Susana altered the balance of his mental and emotional state. This undercurrent broke out, erupted, he said, in nightmares; nightmares that kept him up all night, nightmares that brought back the memories of his cruel crimes and the unsettling urges he claims he always sought to control; nightmares in which he now said he heard the screams of his victims. Caputo couldn't sleep, and found that he could no longer live with himself or his past. He couldn't lie anymore.

To escape the pain, Ricardo Caputo—who hung on to his latest wife and family for two years in Mexico, again under an assumed name—turned to the response that had become the habit of his adult lifetime. He disappeared.

He was running from his past—and, it seemed, he was trying to avoid a more destructive future. But where was he to run *to*? Torn by the threat of losing his family—and fearing what he might again become if left to his own devices, Caputo sought solace and intervention on familiar territory; ironically, it was the place where his problems came to seed—his home.

It was on January 18, 1994 when he appeared on the doorstep of his mother, Alicia de Pinto's home, telling her of his desperate straits. He had to get everything off his chest, confront his past, he explained, and seek out the caliber and amount of professional help he never received enough of in the past in order to completely overcome his inner torments. The voices he heard were no longer those "demanding blood." They were the voices of his victims, and they were haunting his every waking moment. They were also driving this multiple killer out of the shadows he successfully lived in for more than twenty years and into such a state that he knew he had no choice—but to surrender.

A call went out to a prominent lawyer who might be able to assist in handling Caputo's complicated plight. It was attorney Mario Luquez who agreed to see Caputo and discuss the case. Luquez said in an account in the *New York Times*, "He came to my office and started telling me what he had done, and I just could not believe him at first. I thought he was the greatest storyteller in the world. But he kept coming back to talk for so many days, insisting he wanted to give himself up. He was desperate."

Luquez had heard enough in those several meetings to realize that this situation was not only going to be complex, but it was going to require another skilled expert to help sort things out. Caputo's current state—his increased agitation and his desire for action—created an urgency, but became a temporary impediment in communicating, in credible fashion, what he wanted and needed the attorney to know. His accounts of the murders and the revelations of his confused mental state had been coming out in a jumble of words and emotions, the story incredible enough without having unnecessary hurdles blocking its way. Luquez knew just the person who could make sense out of all this. He reached out for assistance from his trusted colleague Dr. Fernando Linares. And Linares, with very little information, followed through on the recommendation of his friend.

The first fateful meeting between Caputo and Linares occurred in the doctor's office. After the introductions, Caputo did not hesitate in making his urgent appeal.

"I've got to turn myself in," he kept repeating in impeccable, exquisite Castilian Spanish. "It's the appropriate way to do it. Time is passing and I have a lot to tell. The families are going to feel better. I want to remediate the pain of the victims' families."

In the next few weeks the psychiatrist and the patient met a total of five times, once for as little as an hour, and one marathon session extending beyond five hours. They were all remarkable by virtue of their contents.

"The second time we met," Linares said, "the things he was telling me were so remarkable and complicated I suggested he write them all down."

But it turned out Caputo had already begun doing that. By the time he arranged to see Dr. Linares, he had already filled twenty-five pages of diaries he referred to as his "notebooks," and what he wrote was astonishing. In the fine, steady hand of an educated gentleman, he described the four murders in detail—two in New York (he denies involvement in the Jacqueline Bernard murder), one in San Francisco, and one in Mexico—and he tried hard to recall his mental state in the period surrounding each murder. His recollections varied.

"There were lagoons of recollections," Dr. Linares said of the diaries. "He said he wrote them to save time. Sometimes he was vague, but mostly he was extremely detailed about everything he'd done."

Caputo explained that the urges and demons were upon him again, just as they'd been when he was a much younger man. Four times, he said, his violent explosions resulted in the murder of young women with whom he'd been in love. It all happened a long time ago, he explained, the last murder seventeen years ago. But they happened. The psychiatrist was amazed at how much Caputo wanted to be believed.

According to the account in the *Times*, Caputo described "broad lines" appearing before his eyes when he was overwhelmed, and voices within demanding "[my] blood." He said there were extended periods of calm in his life—when, for example, he was in a therapeutic relationship or in some other form of psychiatric care, or when he married and immersed himself in family life. The disturbances, the "agitations," were at their most acute just before he killed, and as a killer, by his own description, he was merciless and unspeakably cruel.

Of Natalie Brown's murder, he wrote, "I can't remember clearly what was happening then, except that I was hearing the voices, the shouting, and saw many wide lines. I don't remember anything else."

Caputo claimed that his mental state churned when he began to feel pressured in a relationship, and the more that was demanded of him, the more he sought to extricate himself. This self-view, however, seems to directly contradict what he told police after Brown's killing. At the time, he said he was upset because she said she wanted to move on with her life, and she hinted at another boyfriend. *She* was ending the relationship with *him*. Police officials describe a similar scenario in the subsequent murders—Caputo couldn't handle rejection and the idea of his plans going up in smoke. The diaries, they would assume, reflected his twisted version of events, in which he blamed the victim and turned the situation inside out.

Caputo said he developed a romantic relationship with Dr. Judith Becker, and that he spent weekends at her Yonkers apartment when he obtained "furloughs" from the Manhattan Psychiatric Center. But the relationship with Becker, he wrote in his diaries, began to erode what for him had been "almost a normal mental state." He claimed that "she began to require a lot of sex from me, and I began to change." He saw the lines again, heard the voices again. And killed again.

He wrote that he was hearing the voices "more frequently" in the days leading up to Easter Sunday, 1975. That's when Barbara Ann Taylor was found dead in her apartment.

And the situation worsened two years later, when he killed Laura Gomez. He wrote of those days in Mexico City, "My depressive state is getting worse, and I am constantly hearing voices, shouting, and seeing lines. I am desperate."

He also admitted to a collection of three separate and conflicting personalities. "Frank" was described in his diaries as the man who knew how to make and handle money. "Robert" was charismatic, a family man. And it was "Richard" who was "weak and sick, like a kid playing with a ball, playing in the street." When "Richard" dominated, Ricardo Caputo killed.

Dr. Linares listened and read, and suggested a preliminary diagnosis of schizophrenia. Here was this
man, admitting to a level of inhumanity reached by
only the most notorious figures from history, seeming in his proud bearing and cooperative manner to
be the last person in the world who would get into
any trouble.

"He was formal and obedient," Dr. Linares recalled, "doing whatever was asked of him. Making a
diagnosis is very hard in cases like this, because you
don't see the man when he is sick. You see him when
he's well and merely recollecting what he was. Sometimes he was quite well when he had these flashes of
memory, and he'd be sickened by the kind of man
who would do those things." And here he was, in a
doctor's office, confessing with an urgency that was
quite authentic. "In his sick state," Dr. Linares said,
"he would never have submitted."

Back in 1972, while in psychiatric detention following the murder of Natalie Brown, Caputo supposedly
told a counselor at Matteawan State Hospital that if
he ever escaped, he'd "go to the hills and hide in a
cave." Perhaps Caputo saw himself as a gaucho from
the Argentinean pampa, the vagabond cowboy of legend who rode the open rangelands indifferent to
hardship, in need only of solitude. If that was his self-
view, or represented a significant part of it, then
Caputo surely did encompass more than one personality. Because it seemed that he also craved affection
and attention and was terrified of rejection and indif-

ference. The confessor in Dr. Linares's office was riven with remorse, or appeared to be; certainly, by coming in voluntarily and stating that he would surrender, he was declaring an end to his life "in the hills."

As Dr. Linares continued his sessions with the patient, he tried, along with the attorney Luquez, to work out the logistics of a surrender. But Argentinean officials rebuffed their offer, which proposed incarceration in a local psychiatric institution. After all, the officials pointed out, there were no warrants of any kind in Argentina against one Ricardo Silvio Caputo, and they wanted no part of a surrender scenario that would bring shame on a country whose thirty-two million residents saw themselves as European as opposed to American, who smiled on their own Buenos Aires as the "Paris of South America." Luquez seemed to bear out that sentiment when he told the *Times,* "People cannot take in the dimensions of what he has done. This kind of case has never been seen here before." The message, then, to Caputo was clear: surrender somewhere else.

The lawyer and the psychiatrist went back to Caputo's mother. She contacted her older son, Alberto, in New York City. He agreed to make the arrangements. Through friends and recommendations, he hired Park Avenue attorney Michael Kennedy, who had a reputation for handling cases too hot or too big for the average attorney.

* * *

Weeks after his return to his home, the stage was set for Caputo to return to American soil. On March 8, he was secretly hustled out of Argentina, accompanied on a plane bound for Kennedy Airport in New York by his lawyer's private investigators. As he left his native land for perhaps the final time, Caputo may not have been aware that the activities there ironically reflected the mission on which he had embarked. In March, the city of Mendoza marks both happy and sad occasions in its illustrious history. Residents spend months preparing for La Vendimia, the annual feast that celebrates the abundant and lucrative grape harvest. At the same time, the city acknowledges a commemoration of a darker and more solemn kind: a memorial service honoring the ten thousand people who perished in the tragic earthquake of 1861.

In parallel fashion, here was Ricardo Caputo, ready to confess—to surrender—to purge himself of his own demons. It's an endeavor some may consider honorable. But as Caputo demonstrated so fatefully in his past, a dark side seemed almost always to accompany his attempts at success. And the dark side of these admissions would soon encompass the families of his victims. For Ricardo Caputo's re-emergence back into their lives would inevitably return them to the pain and horror they tried to bury with the loved ones who died at his hand.

CHAPTER SEVENTEEN

State Police Senior Investigator Kevin Cavanaugh looked at his watch again and resisted the urge to ask his driver to lean on the horn. The only thing worse than driving into Manhattan on the Long Island Expressway, he thought, was having to do it in the rain. And now, just past midday on March 9, 1994, it was raining hard. Traffic was hardly moving and his patience was beginning to wear thin. It had been a waiting game for a week, waiting for a phone call and the go signal as he remained on standby at the New York State Trooper Headquarters at Republic Airport in Farmingdale, Long Island. Finally, the night before, the call had come. A former colleague, George Gross, was working as a private investigator for a flamboyant, media-savvy Manhattan attorney named Michael Kennedy. "Come in to Kennedy's office tomorrow," Gross had said in the late night phone call, "that thing we're talking about is going to go down about four-thirty or five in the afternoon."

The "thing" about to go down was the surrender of a subject who'd been a fugitive for twenty years, an Argentinean named Ricardo Caputo. Cavanaugh had spent the week learning what he could about Caputo. It was a strange case and Cavanaugh was receiving information in bits and pieces from all over the continent. Cavanaugh's boss, Captain Walter Heesch, who commands Long Island's sixty-five State Police investigators, told him initially that Gross called on behalf of the lawyer Kennedy, but that he was playing it very close to the vest. All Gross had said, in fact, was that this guy Caputo was a long-time fugitive who was planning to return from an unnamed country to turn himself in. Cryptic, Heesch thought, but intriguing to say the least. "It's kind of an unusual circumstance for a person after many years to even want to turn himself in," he recalled later. "We have a number of people on our Twelve Most Wanted list who we haven't found; usually you only find them accidentally by running into them in some other incident, and when you run their names or prints you catch them. But here was a case of a guy coming forward, after all these years . . ."

"We didn't really know anything about the suspect at first," Cavanaugh would explain. "It was just an old case, a real old one, and we had to start digging around a little just to find out why he was wanted." Heesch encouraged the digging and, by the time Gross called with the final details of the surrender, he and his men knew exactly why Caputo was wanted, knew how badly he was wanted, and knew they were walking into a case—or, walking back into a case—

that would explode on the front page of every newspaper and at the top of every newscast.

Part of that certainty was rooted in the simple fact that Michael Kennedy had signed on to the case. Kennedy, who had just wrapped up the loose ends of Ivana Trump's highly publicized divorce settlement with her ex-husband, New York tycoon Donald Trump, was the Park Avenue lawyer personified, and a frequent presence in headline cases. Kennedy played the media like his personal fiddle, and no doubt had a game plan for Ricardo Caputo.

Then there was the suspect's brother, Alberto Caputo, who'd retained Kennedy in the first place. In a week's time Heesch's men had learned that Alberto Caputo could well afford Kennedy's steep fees. He'd worked himself up to become chief executive officer of Lexington Photo Labs, a lucrative commercial venture in Manhattan, and it provided him with a life of comfort and privilege in Fieldston, a private enclave in the exclusive section of Riverdale. There were also the other properties, including significant acreage in upstate New York. References in their prominent social circle led them to Michael Kennedy.

Ricardo Caputo might be a stone-cold killer, Heesch thought, but whatever he's up to now, there's money and power behind him.

Driving into Manhattan, Cavanaugh lightly ran his fingers over the folder in his lap. His computer searches had spit out a wealth of information on the subject he was expecting to arrest in a few hours.

Caputo's name appeared on local arrest warrants for murder from Nassau County on Long Island and from the city of Yonkers in Westchester County. There was the FBI warrant citing Caputo for murder in San Francisco and unlawful flight to avoid prosecution, and paperwork generated by his violent escape from an INS detention center in El Paso, Texas. Finally, Caputo was listed as the prime suspect in a 1983 murder in Manhattan. Busy boy, Cavanaugh thought. "We knew we had a very bad individual on our hands. I just wanted to get him back in the system where he belongs so he's not out there killing other people."

Cavanaugh had planned his operation carefully, right down to the smallest details. His team included six of his top investigators, now traveling with him in two different cars in case one broke down or got into an accident. He opted for the additional manpower because of the suspect's violent background and the possibility that as a successful fugitive, he might at the last minute have a change of heart and attempt to escape. Seven men total, two cars, Cavanaugh had decided: nothing to chance. His own white Dodge Dynasty would transport the suspect, with a maroon Dodge as the backup. Cavanaugh also personally inspected the contents of the modest gym bag packed especially for this arrest. In it was the so-called Violent Prisoner Restraining Kit, whose design and purpose were brutally simple and unequivocal: it was a beltlike device consisting of handcuffs attached to the belt by short lengths of chain and leg irons bound to each other and double-secured to the waist. By allowing its wearer to take steps no longer than twelve to sixteen inches, it did its job of limiting movement.

And, of course, every man in Cavanaugh's team carried his nine-millimeter automatic.

Cavanaugh shifted impatiently in his seat as the two-car caravan navigated the last constipated miles of the expressway toward the Queens Midtown Tunnel, and he wondered to himself where he read that a commuter from Long Island who drives the expressway every day over a whole career might spend between one and two years of his life just sitting on the highway. That sounds about right, Cavanaugh thought as he watched the car barely moving in front of him. He was just glad he didn't have to do it often. In this case, all he wanted to do was get in, get the guy, get him back out to the Island, and process him back into the system.

But first he had to get the guy.

The team pulled up to 425 Park Avenue, in the heart of midtown Manhattan, and parked. Cavanaugh was waiting for one more call from Gross on the car phone and it came at four-thirty sharp. "You and your men can meet me in the ground-floor lobby and I'll escort you up," Gross said. Cavanaugh hung up, selected three men to go with him and instructed three others to stay behind.

Gross was there, as promised, standing in the massive lobby with its slate-gray granite floors and huge modern collage over the reception desk. It was a quiet elevator ride, Cavanaugh fingering the warrants and paperwork in his fat file and wishing like hell the job would go quickly.

But when the elevator came to a stop on the twenty-sixth floor, the doors opened directly into Kennedy's office suite, where an extraordinary scene greeted the investigator and his men. There were television lights all over the place and two cameras from ABC's program "Prime Time Live" recording the arrival of the arresting officers, who found themselves, literally, in the spotlight. Cavanaugh didn't have time to appreciate the posh interior of the office suite—the black leather couch and side chairs, the Persian rug atop a plush green carpet, the lush floral displays and graceful plants, the subtle track lighting and gorgeous prints and paintings, the paneling and cabinetry and bookshelves in different hues of the richest woods. All Cavanaugh saw was the lights, and he blinked hard against them. The whole scene was being taped!

Kennedy approached him, extending a hand. His blond hair was going white, his usually flying eyebrows quiet and serious as he greeted the investigator. He explained that his client had just given an interview to the senior correspondent of "Prime Time," Chris Wallace, an exclusive interview in which he confessed to the four murders he said he'd committed. Wallace had spent a good hour with Caputo before Gross had made the phone call to the investigators waiting outside the building. He was an ace reporter and had a well-deserved national reputation to prove it; typically, his first questions to Caputo had been as direct as gunfire.

CHRIS WALLACE: You have been accused of killing victim after victim over the years. Did you kill Natalie Brown?

RICARDO CAPUTO: Yes, sir.

CW: Did you kill Judith Becker?

RC: Yes, sir.

CW: Did you kill Barbara Taylor?

RC: Yes, sir.

CW: Did you kill Laura Gomez?

RC: Yes, sir.

In the rest of the interview the confessing killer, by turns, apologized to his victims' families, nearly succumbed to the apparent emotion of the moment, and articulated his (and his lawyer's) defense strategy.

"Now I understand the pain I caused," he explained wearily in so soft a voice that Wallace strained to hear, "when I did that to those people. But I was sincerely sick, I was not a criminal . . ."

Wallace later explained, "Michael Kennedy decided it would be in Mr. Caputo's interest to have him tell his story before he was taken into custody. My sense of it was that Kennedy was primarily concerned that Caputo get treatment and not just be thrown into a jail cell, so that he could, to a degree, control the circumstances under which Caputo was taken into custody. Then he could give the indication that this was a sick man who did need help and was giving himself up—not just that he'd been arrested. He wanted the story out that Caputo was turning himself over because he wanted help and thought it might lead to treatment. "Prime Time" had had some dealings with Michael Kennedy on a variety of past stories, and I think he felt we were a broadcast that would do a fair and honest job of reporting this story. He got in touch with us and asked if we wanted to do the interview . . . and that we could be here when he was taken into custody."

But beyond dangling the bait, Kennedy hadn't given "Prime Time" much more than he'd allowed Gross to give the State Police. "He was quite secretive about where Caputo was," Wallace recalled, "what country, when he was coming in. We were only told about it several days before . . ." One of Wallace's concerns—and one of his own network's concerns—was that at the time they were negotiating the terms of the exclusive interview, nobody, literally nobody, had Caputo in custody. "This was a man who we believed was a confessed multiple killer. We didn't want to be doing anything that could in any way contribute to the possibility that he might be in custody, and then escape, and then be back out on the street. So Kennedy hired private detectives who stayed with Caputo from the moment he stepped off the plane and onto New York City soil. So he was, in a sense, in custody . . ."

Wallace had a few minutes to study Caputo before the actual on-camera interview began, and to add his own direct observations to the details from the hastily assembled file his staff had given him. "He was very stressed, clearly a very troubled man—at one point during the interview, in fact, he felt he was being overwhelmed by his emotions. But I was also struck at how composed he was." A schizophrenic, Wallace's notes told him.

Now it was Kevin Cavanaugh's turn to take center stage. As one of his investigators snapped the handcuffs onto Caputo's wrists, Cavanaugh handed the arrest warrants to the killer's lawyer. There was no need to read the suspect his Miranda rights; the surrender had been effected according to an agreement drawn up by his own lawyer. Cavanaugh was determined to carry out his job with cool and calm professionalism, despite the distraction of the TV lights and cameras, but he was aware of them too. Thank God, he thought, I'm wearing my good gray suit. That, combined with his trim build, reddish-brown hair, paisley tie, and crisp white shirt made for a nice appearance for the camera. But that was the furthest thing from his mind as he moved to take his prisoner by the elbow. But Alberto Caputo stepped in first, speaking quietly to his shorter brother. Then Kennedy touched Ricardo Caputo on the shoulder and drew near. He handed his client his black leather jacket, and once Caputo put it on, spoke quietly—the camera's microphone recording it all.

"They're taking you into custody now, Ricardo. You'll have an opportunity to meet with me later." Caputo looked up meekly and said, "Okay." Kennedy gave his shoulder a final squeeze. "You take care of yourself, all right?"

The arresting team then surrounded Caputo and escorted him through the ornate lobby and out onto rainy Park Avenue, the unusual scene turning heads as the group walked by. Caputo was placed into the white Dynasty and sat hunched in the backseat. It was an even longer drive back out to Long Island, with the rush-hour traffic this time. Caputo said nothing during the tedious ride; Cavanaugh asked him no questions.

When they all got back to State Police Headquarters in Farmingdale, Caputo was placed in a small windowless office and remained chained and shackled while the processing team sent fresh fingerprints off for verification of the subject's identity. It was a process that at times could take as long as eight hours, but in this instance the answer came back in less than two hours. Ricardo Caputo was who he said he was.

Cavanaugh had tried some small talk with the suspect sitting in chains while the fingerprint check was still under way. Caputo may have looked sympathetic, but he was smart enough to stick to what he'd said for the television cameras—and what he'd said to his psychiatrist back in Mendoza, Argentina: he killed four women, he didn't know what he was doing when he did it, he was sorry, he wanted forgiveness from the victims' families.

At ten P.M. two cars, one official, one unmarked, transported Caputo fourteen miles to the Mineola headquarters of the Nassau County Police Department. And, by that hour, Caputo's attorney had already set the wheels in motion for a massive media blitz. The interview and confession for "Prime Time Live" wouldn't be broadcast for at least another week, but the lawyer knew that—had planned it that way—and was already in touch with print and radio reporters whose stories would saturate the newspapers and the airwaves within days. A DRIFTER'S TALE OF SERIAL DEATH, trumpeted the headline in the *New York Times*. *Newsday*'s come-on was, KILLER SWEET-TALKED VICTIMS. The page-one header in the *Chicago Tribune* was, TWENTY YEAR WORLDWIDE CHASE ENDS WITH SURRENDER OF SERIAL KILLER. In San Francisco, where Barbara Ann Taylor had been stomped to death nineteen years earlier, the *Chronicle*'s headline was, A CHARMER AND A HUSTLER—FOUR WOMEN ARE DEAD.

Laced throughout every dispatch were generous quotes from Michael Kennedy. He'd allowed his client to make one carefully controlled statement in a single interview on a national broadcast; beyond that statement, the Park Avenue lawyer alone would speak for his client and for his client's case, and speak he did. "Mr. Caputo is a certified schizophrenic," he told reporters in his nearly immutable mantra, "whose psychotic and normal personalities have now informed one another to such an extent that he is able to recognize his old illness and seek help for it." It was a smart ploy, portraying killer as victim.

He knew all too well that reporters would now be running back to the victims' families and friends, among whom word had spread quickly that the killer was in jail, in America, and had confessed. The pain of reopened wounds was as obvious and as predictable as some of the reactions; vocal, stoked with renewed anger, and, for some, just short of violent. There were some expressions of shock that Caputo was still alive, and some of satisfaction that he was again behind bars; but mostly, the families and friends of the dead women cursed the killer. Several said it was a shame he'd turned himself in in New York, a state that had switched off its electric chair and deemed capital punishment illegal. Kennedy was surprised by none of the reaction; he knew that all he needed to do was to convince a jury, even a single juror, that his client was as sick as he claimed to be, and he could mark his representation of Ricardo Caputo in the victory column. He would be doing his client's bidding, on terms the lawyer himself would dictate.

As the clock struck midnight, that client was sitting on the edge of a bed in a six-by-eight-foot prison cell in the Nassau County Jail, the same jail where he'd been held twenty-three years ago after he'd fatally stabbed his twenty-year-old girlfriend, Natalie Brown. He was due in court the next day to face a reprise of the murder charge for which he'd never stood trial.

Unless he entered a guilty plea, which would seal his fate for the rest of his life, Ricardo Caputo knew a trial was certainly inevitable although its outcome unknown. With that distressing prospect, Caputo lay back on the thin mattress and tried to sleep, but couldn't as his thoughts zipped back and forth from past to present. Only twenty-four hours ago, he thought, he'd been home and still free in Argentina. Now he was behind bars, with the odds stacked against the likelihood that he would ever experience freedom again. His attorney and his family were hard at work putting together a scenario and a defense that would offer him a fighting chance of staying out of prison. If he was convicted of the crime free and clear, he faced the prospect of spending the rest of his life in the correctional system, a system of concrete walls and metal bars and a permanent routine that never included the possibility of breathing the air outside the restricting gates. But there was another option that provided a glimmer—although a faint one—of hope. If Ricardo Caputo was found not guilty by reason of insanity, he would have to be confined to a mental institution. But in that institution, he would receive treatment, and if that treatment was successful, there was the possibility—perhaps remote, but a possibility nonetheless—that at some point he could be released. But Caputo couldn't allow himself that kind of optimism at the present time. His immediate future was an appearance before a judge, an appearance that meant exposing the face of a killer that had been successfully hidden for more than two decades. It was a face the public—and the press—was eager to see.

CHAPTER EIGHTEEN

The courthouse-beat reporters had already been alerted the night before. "Heads up" was the message, from Ed Grilli, the district attorney's spokesman, "action in Judge Dunne's courtroom in the morning." Lieutenant Paul Kunz and Captain Pete Matuzza of the Nassau County Police Department called over to the press room; get your cameras to the back of headquarters—this is going to be a good "perp walk."

A press corps that shares a single beat is something like a family, which is to say that on the easy stuff, everybody gets along and helps out. The bare bones of the Caputo story—a brutal killer surrendering after twenty years on the lam—was an easy hit, a can't miss headline, and the reporters milled around their press room in the Supreme Court Building in Mineola and wondered about the latest "monster" they would all soon be seeing for the first time. Winter had returned with a vengeance on the morning of March 10 after the rains of the day before, and the dozen or so reporters in the press room sipped coffee and made their requisite phone calls as they geared up for what was going to turn out to be the story of the day. Some debated when to make the run through the harsh cold winds to begin the ritual stakeout, others filled out applications for audio, video, and photographic coverage of the proceedings. Judge Dunne's courtroom was small, they all knew; it was going to be a scramble for seats. But since it was just an appearance on an arrest warrant, maybe the judge would allow the overflow, if there were any, to occupy the jury box seats; it had happened before.

The reporters who were on the ball had already asked their newsrooms to begin a search on anything and everything on file about Ricardo Caputo, and hours before the arraignment, the material started coming in. There were clips about the Natalie Brown murder—and photos of Caputo from that time. Those photos, from twenty-three years before, revealed a boyishly handsome face framing large brown eyes and long brown swept-back hair above a dimpled square jaw. His good looks were obvious, despite the map of confusion written all over his face. Then other photos were faxed to the press room, photos from the investigations of the subsequent murders. Caputo's hairline was receding over the years, and he was developing a slight paunch. There were clips of stories that quoted police in Yonkers and San Francisco as saying that the killer not only changed his name and address at the drop of a hat, but was also adept at changing his look, even down to the details of gaining or losing weight and removing or adding tattoos. The reporters couldn't wait to get a firsthand look at the man who was returning to the scene of the crime . . . more than two decades later!

If the journalists' speculation about Caputo's court appearance was in especially high gear, it was partly because their tabloid sensibilities had been recently stoked by two concurrent cases involving killers of distinction who'd chosen Long Island as the stage for their particular brands of mayhem. An unemployed gardener described as a classic nerd—Joel Rifkin—had recently confessed to killing at least seventeen prostitutes over a five-year span—saving personal mementos, including teeth and underwear after some of the murders—and an educated black named Colin Ferguson had been arrested after a rush-hour shooting rampage on a homebound Long Island Railroad car. He left six commuters dead and nineteen wounded. They were both multiple murderers, but their cases were vastly different and their personalities a study in contrasts. Rifkin, in every court appearance, was aloof, detached, and uninterested to the point where he sometimes fell asleep during the hearings being held in his case. The burly Ferguson, on the other hand, seemed ready to literally burst out of his prison-issue orange ensemble as he peppered the proceedings in his case with angry outbursts and caustic diatribes. From the reporters' standpoint, both killers were great copy and good running stories.

But now the reporters had new material, this guy named Caputo, who'd brutally killed women he'd been in love with, and they were flat-out hungry with curiosity: What would this killer show of himself? What deadly characteristics would he reveal, or hide?

Apparently, it wasn't just the reporters whose curiosity had been inflamed. The crowd was growing in the central hallway outside Judge Dunne's courtroom, as secretaries and lawyers and assistant D.A.'s, as was the custom, stopped by hoping to steal a few minutes or more from their regular jobs to look in on the most interesting item on the day's docket. Courthouse security made the decision to move the proceedings into a bigger first-floor venue, and by ten in the morning everyone was seated.

Each and every head turned and eyes grew wide as the escorted prisoner shuffled up the side aisle and approached the defense table. The reporters stared blankly as the old equation kicked in again, a surprise every time, though it shouldn't have been; one expects a killer of distinctive brutality to be a larger-than-life demon, but that's rarely the case. Rifkin and Ferguson were the recent examples, and now there was Caputo to repeat the lesson: there is no textbook standard on how such a killer should look. And, often, they look as ordinary and unremarkable as the most ordinary and unremarkable of people.

"We were looking for the Big Bad Wolf," one reporter said, "and here was this little guy . . ."

Caputo was wearing the same jeans, brown work

shoes, and blue-striped shirt he'd worn for the "Prime Time Live" interview the day before, but everything was a little rumpled, his shirt now unbuttoned nearly to his waist and exposing chest hair and a modest gold chain. Reporters were reaching for the likelihood that this alleged ladies' man was dressing the part. But in reality the unkempt look came from sleeping in the same clothes and redressing to cover the handcuffs and leg irons he was required to wear.

What did strike the reporters was the defendant's casual air. He seemed tired and a bit nervous, but also very much in control and at ease. Almost vain, and disturbingly so. One reporter claimed that at one point Caputo glanced around the room and tried to make eye contact with several of the women who were present, offering a small, sad smile.

That wasn't the case when Caputo, just minutes before his court appearance, faced the barrage of clicking cameras and screaming reporters as he walked out of Nassau County Police Headquarters. Police won't admit it, but the "perp-walk" is an opportunity for the press to take a few good shots as a suspect is placed in a police car and transported to jail or court. In Nassau County the routine occurs outside the rear door of headquarters, adjacent to the public parking lot. Ricardo Caputo winced, looked dazed and confused while trying to retain some modicum of composure as reporters strained from their positions behind the barricades. "Why'd you do it?" "What made you kill all these women?"

"Are you really nuts?" Caputo made no response but couldn't get out of the situation any faster since his restraints limited his ability to walk. The subsequent pictures portray a weary man with a lined, time-worn face just a bit too old for his stylish leather jacket.

In court, the proceedings were short and to the point. The only time Caputo spoke was when Judge Dunne asked him two direct questions. Was he in fact Ricardo Silvio Caputo, as identified in Indictment #32240 of 1971 relating to the murder of Natalie Brown; and, was he represented by an attorney? In a voice so small he could not be heard by the reporters sitting a few yards behind him, Caputo answered "yes" to each question.

The assistant district attorney handling the arraignment, Major Offense Bureau Chief George Peck, got down to the nuts and bolts of the case, explaining that this was an arrest warrant dating back to 1975. It took Judge Dunne by surprise as Peck explained that Caputo had been remanded to a mental facility at the time. But if he ever intended to make a display for the press and reveal Caputo's criminal and personal history to the court, including his adoption of various identities and aliases and his two escapes from custody, he wasn't going to get the chance. Caputo's lawyer made it his business to keep the ball in his court. Months before any trial might take place, Michael Kennedy was already setting up the building blocks for an insanity defense.

"Your Honor," he began, "I have a very seriously mentally ill client, and I'm concerned about immediate psychiatric care, immediate evaluation. He's been able to maintain some level of chemical balance regarding his terrible schizophrenia through the use of some medication prescribed for him by another doctor. That medication will be exhausted as of today—he only had two pills as of last night when I surrendered him. So, I'm concerned that he will be subjected to some very serious additional emotional trauma if he doesn't receive immediate medical and psychiatric attention."

Judge Dunne wrapped the hearing in a matter of minutes, ordering Caputo back to the Nassau County Jail and giving all sides a week to discuss the psychiatric evaluations that might be appropriate and useful as the case went forward. Caputo was led from the courtroom wordlessly, showing no emotion.

Once outside the courtroom, it was time for Michael Kennedy to do what he did best—take control. He never flinched as the reporters rushed toward him. He strode calmly and confidently down the hallway as a cluster of microphones and cameras grew in front of his regal, imposing figure. The lawyer had been through it before, and now spoke in deliberate tones as he adjusted his wire-rimmed glasses, his shock of thick white hair glistening in the lights and his clear blue eyes looking directly at each questioner.

"Why did he turn himself in *now?*" one reporter pressed. Kennedy answered slowly. "It's not so much the killing as it is the *echoes* of screams and violence, bits and pieces of it, and he's seeing lines and dots before his eyes. He feels great remorse—*his word*—great sadness about what he's done and about the terrible pain he's inflicted on the victims and on the victims' families. Now that he's a parent himself, he appreciated to an even greater degree the terrible pain he caused these families."

No, the lawyer said: he didn't see his client as a criminal.

"He belongs in a medical facility, a high-security custodial medical facility where we can all be assured —and he can be assured—that he cannot harm himself or anyone else."

But the reporters pressed on, demanding to know more about Caputo's past, about the chunks of his life that were unaccounted for. They were already picking up bits and pieces from law enforcement officials, and within days their sources would begin providing tantalizing tips suggesting the defendant in the wrinkled striped shirt was more than just a nutcase—more evil, more cunning, more tailored to screaming headlines. Kennedy was prepared for their persistence; he deflected the questions as premature—after all, he'd just met his client for the first time the day before—and promised he'd pass along what he learned as he learned it.

And, seemingly true to his word, when Kennedy returned to court for the next scheduled hearing a week later, he brought Caputo's brother and sister-in-law with him.

There wasn't a reporter in Judge Dunne's courtroom the day of that second hearing who knew anything about Alberto and Kim Caputo except that the couple lived in the Bronx. But their appearance stated clearly that they were not from the poor side of the tracks, and their carriage—a striking couple almost gliding into the courtroom—conveyed a sense of style as well as wealth. Alberto's gray-flecked hair was combed back carefully, Kim's brunette tresses fell softly and perfectly to her shoulders. "A symphony in beige," one reporter remarked about their elegant and understated clothing. And a distinct contrast to the now thoroughly disheveled defendant whose circumstances seemed worlds away from the couple holding hands and staring grimly at the proceedings from the first spectator row.

The Caputos were undoubtedly in court not just to show moral support for a troubled relative, but to bolster the sympathetic image being carefully constructed by attorney Kennedy. They listened attentively as Judge Dunne ordered a new psychiatric examination to determine the defendant's current fitness to stand trial, nodding together in agreement over their belief that Ricardo suffered from a debilitating illness.

When the hearing ended, the Caputos left the courtroom, and when the reporters converged on them, handed out Xerox copies of a two-page typewritten statement. They tried to duck questions by beating a hasty retreat to the courthouse elevators, but the elevators, whose slowness usually drew curses from reporters, now became a friend of the press by denying the Caputos their escape.

"What about Ricardo's past!" the reporters shouted as they circled the couple. To Alberto, one asked, "What did you know about your brother's activities?" Alberto and his wife answered politely and concisely, mindful of keeping to the statement they'd just handed out. "We are now confident," Alberto said several times, "that my brother is getting the help he needs." He urged the reporters to consult the typed statement in their hands, a statement that he said included the answers the family was able to give. No, Alberto insisted, the family "had not heard from Alberto in twenty years. We thought he was probably dead. We were shocked to find out that he'd surfaced in Argentina and was now pleading for help." And Ricardo needed and deserved the help he was seeking, Alberto said again and again. "Please, read the statement."

In fact, the "statement" raised more questions than it answered, offering at best a skewed and partial glimpse of a childhood shrouded in mystery. But at least it was a first look at Ricardo Caputo's roots—the version according to Alberto, to be sure. The two pages contained ten, single-spaced paragraphs. Although it was released on behalf of the couple, it was written from Kim Caputo's point of view.

* * *

These last eight weeks we have lived through the most difficult and confusing days. It is still hard to believe any of this is happening. Alberto had thought his brother was probably dead. After no word from him for over twenty years, the phone call for help from Argentina was an absolute shock that paralyzed every other aspect of our lives. Our next move would be vital because the fate of someone else might lie in our hands. We had to do something right away.

We called Michael Kennedy, who arranged for a surrender in his office, and Alberto flew to Argentina, picked up his distressed brother and returned to New York with him. There were many times during the trip that he was worried about Ricardo's behavior, about the plan being thwarted, about being kidnapped or ambushed by authorities in Latin America, or even being intercepted by the FBI before they would meet Mr. Kennedy and his detectives.

Wednesday March 9, we sat in Mr. Kennedy's office listening to Ricardo's story. Everyone present was moved to tears. This man was so sick, so sorry and so ready for whatever was to make him and others safe from his horrible nightmare.

That evening when I watched my husband's face as he spoke to "Prime Time" reporters, I saw a different person. Suddenly all the inexplicable elements of his character were clear to me. I was overwhelmed. At that moment I knew we were experiencing an incredible lesson. Something that we could share and help others with.

From tragedy comes some vital truth. The crucial thing that is born of this matter is that Ricardo could have been helped long ago and none of these deaths would have come to pass. He begged for help many times and was left alone with his terrible illness and the devices that he created to deal with the pain and abuse of his childhood.

Ricardo Caputo was abandoned as a small boy. He was raped. He was beaten. He was ignored when he begged for help. Turned away from his own home, he went alone to a mental hospital in Mendoza, Argentina, a hospital called "Sause" which, when translated, means "Weeping Willow." No one knew how to help him there. He joined the priesthood looking for salvation, but the love and understanding he needed eluded him. The pressures of his mental disease grew more and more intense. He lived with his hallucinations and lies, hiding from his past. He clearly remembers his love relationships but cannot understand why they ended in such violence. He turned himself in after committing his first murder here on Long Island and was treated so loosely that he was on the street before two years were up.

Not once in twenty years did any authority question his identity. He could walk on the streets in Hawaii like a tourist. He was able to travel from one country to another without being caught. The blood on his hands, the screams in his head, the hallucinations that blinded him from his deeds seemed to have veiled him from the world. He not only was left alone with his disease, he had become invisible.

Why has he turned himself in after all this time? We think it must be that the love and support of his present wife has given him the peace of mind and freedom from the fear of being rejected. The comfort of their relationship has made him visible again. His conscience has returned.

Ricardo is emerging again and he has grown so full with remorse that he couldn't face his wife. He couldn't stand lying to his children any more. He had only one choice. To turn himself in. To seek forgiveness.

Our deepest sympathies go to the families of the victims. As parents ourselves, we can only imagine the anger and emptiness in their homes. We know that it will be almost impossible for them to forgive but we urge them to find meaning in all of this. Hate and fear of those that are deranged won't change what happened. We can save lives though. Ricardo Caputo's tragedy will remind us what happens to children who are neglected and abused. We must be aware of early signs of mental illness and listen to our children's pleas for help.

In the next two weeks the reporters working the Caputo case learned that law enforcement officials who'd been tracking the killer for two decades believed that he'd stayed in touch with his family. This was a cunning man, they said, who was constantly on the move, surfacing in dozens of locations in and out of the country. They told reporters Caputo had likely traveled between the U.S. and Argentina several times, and that he may have contacted his mother or brother.

The picture of the Caputo family drawn by law enforcement sources was of a clannish bunch, the mother in Argentina claiming without fail that she knew nothing, and the brother in Riverdale saying all he knew was that Ricardo was dead.

Still, there was the "troubled childhood" aspect to the story, and it wouldn't go away. Investigative sources said Caputo used his "troubled childhood" as a ploy to win over the women he eventually murdered, that he was nothing more than a cunning social climber who targeted upscale women sympathetic to his tale and eager, despite their better judgment, to help him overcome his abusive and poverty-stricken past. The lead investigator on one of the murders told a reporter that Caputo's victims were eerily alike in many ways, starting with their appearance as slim, pretty brunettes. Each of them was also a "highly intelligent, compassionate woman," the investigator said, "with an abiding concern for the underdog. He fit them perfectly. They fit each other."

Ricardo Caputo's decision to surrender awakened in a single stroke a sleeping giant of a case, and its ripple effect was just beginning to spread. The first notable shock wave hit his wife, Susana, head-on.

Caputo told "Prime Time" during his historic confession and surrender that he didn't call her until a week before he was set to return to New York, and that when he told her what he was doing, she didn't know what to think. For more than two months the mother of his children had been living in confusion and fear, worrying that perhaps he'd been kidnapped. When he finally did contact her, he told her the truth—all the terrible, terrible truths.

"He told me he had killed four people," Susana said through an interpreter on "Prime Time." "I said, 'What are you saying?' and he said, 'No, Susie, you have to know. This is the truth, and you have to know it.' "

Producer Peter Sparrow of "America's Most Wanted" already had inklings that the killer had resurfaced in his homeland. "We got two anonymous tips saying he'd come back to Mendoza. The first call, checking the logs against his later confession, came in three days after he arrived there in January. We sent the info to the FBI."

The FBI subsequently made calls to the victims' families. Vera Taylor, the mother of San Francisco murder victim Barbara Ann Taylor, said the bureau contacted her the night before Caputo returned to New York. Ed Brown, the brother of Caputo's girlfriend and first victim, Natalie Brown, says he was notified before that by a producer from "America's

Most Wanted" and by retired Yonkers Police Detective Joe Surlack, who never got over the frustration of having failed to reel in the killer of Judy Becker.

As reporters scrambled to find out whatever they could about this admitted killer, and surviving relatives steeled themselves against the tortuous journey they'd be bound to take back into their past, the law enforcement community began dusting off their files and refreshing their recollections. They wanted to make sure that their cases were going to stick against a man who seemed protected, almost Teflon-coated from capture, for more than twenty years.

CHAPTER NINETEEN

In the aftermath of Ricardo Caputo's confession and surrender, there are cops and citizens on red alert in Yonkers, San Francisco, Mexico City, and on Long Island, the venues where he struck; they are not only grabbing at memories, but facts and case files that may have become fuzzy around the edges, but which will soon zoom into sharp focus as the criminal justice system swings into action against this multiple killer. After all, multiple killer, multiple cases. Long Island authorities get first crack at him, and they plan on going to trial. But the questions that loom largest are: How will that trial play out, and can Caputo and a clever lawyer end-run the system?

After Nassau County, Westchester County gets the next at-bat and will attempt to bring Ricardo Caputo to justice for the Yonkers murder of Judy Becker. Assistant District Attorney Jeannine Pirro has jurisdiction in the Becker case and says, "We lodged a detainer as soon as we were aware he'd turned himself in. We're in the process of putting together an indictment, and it's our intention to try Caputo as soon as he's tried in Nassau County." Pirro concedes it's always more difficult to put together an older case than a fresh one. "This is a case, the Becker murder, that was investigated almost twenty years ago, and we are attempting even now to gather witnesses and evidence in a way that will strongly support the handing up of an indictment." Pirro says defense attorney Michael Kennedy's media blitz won't affect how her case is constructed. "We'll try the case the same way," she insists, "irrespective of whether or not the defendant seeks to gain some benefit as a result of having gone on national television. But as far as we're concerned, we've got a job to do. We're going to meet the elements of the crime and we're going to prove our case beyond a reasonable doubt."

Four years later, a Westchester County grand jury indicted Caputo for the murder of Judy Becker. Pirro said at that time that Caputo's televised confession "was the hook we needed to tie him to the Becker slaying."

It helps to have detectives who never let a case go, even though it's long gone and sometimes forgotten in the public's eye. And it's not an infrequent occurrence when detectives grow attached, or something short of fixated, on a case that didn't end in what they consider satisfactory fashion. For them, the best of all possible worlds is an arrest and subsequent conviction on the charges. If that doesn't take place, there may be a feeling of closure if the suspect is known to be incarcerated as a result of a separate, independent case. There's also finality if or when it's learned that the defendant has died.

Then there is the scenario spelled out by Caputo's current situation; the killer comes forward, even confesses, but short of a guilty plea, must stand trial. And the combination of a jury system and a good lawyer more often than not constitutes a roll of the dice.

In Yonkers, there are detectives—since retired—who still have Judith Becker's murder fresh in their minds. Their expertise and almost innate knowledge of the case will no doubt augment that of their counterparts who inherited the bulging file.

And in this case, the victim's family may prove to be very helpful. The Beckers, who remained ever vigilant and worked hard with and independently of police in trying to track down their daughter's killer, are still outspoken and supportive of the case. Even months after the murder, the Beckers themselves traveled from their Connecticut home to New York City on the chance they'd find someone who could tell them of Caputo's whereabouts. At the time, they took out ads in Spanish language newspapers in their quest for his capture. Mrs. Becker wrote letters demanding answers from New York State mental health officials about Caputo's escape from the Manhattan Psychiatric Center, and years later, she wrote to law enforcement officials in Mexico when Caputo's name surfaced in connection with another grisly killing. No detective worth his or her salt, retired or not, would ever let that kind of persistence and determination go by the boards.

In San Francisco there's a mirror image of what has been taking place three thousand miles east. Police Inspector Earl Sanders has pushed the file on Barbara Ann Taylor's murder to the front of his desk. Two months after Caputo's surrender, the veteran detective began a thorough review process after sewing up the final details of another high-profile murder investigation in the City by the Bay. It was a politically sensitive case involving the racially motivated death of a young teenager. The department called in its best to handle the investigation, and until that was resolved, Sanders wasn't going to be able to clear his calendar to set aside time for the case he caught almost twenty years ago. He got that time in May when he began to refresh his recollection about Barbara Ann Taylor's gruesome killing. Since then, he's been reaching out to people involved in the case, and he's contemplating a future trip to New York to speak to law enforcement officials involved here.

Authorities in Nassau County have also been scrambling to pull together their own even older case. Natalie Brown was stabbed to death in 1971. Were the witnesses still around, including the detectives who'd handled that case? What about the records?

Martha Haesloop, the law secretary for Judge John Dunne, made her early calls to the county clerk's office on the courthouse's second floor. She knew, even before they answered the phone, that it wasn't likely she'd find the Natalie Brown case folder there.

"As it turned out," she explained, "the clerk said he'd have to re-create the file from microfilm."

Ed Grilli, the spokesman for Nassau County District Attorney Dennis Dillon, knew they'd also have to locate and produce the grand jury minutes and psychiatric reports from 1971. At that time, Ricardo Caputo had been indicted on a single count of "intentional murder," and following that, doctors determined that Caputo was incompetent to stand trial.

"All those files," Grilli said with a grimace, "may have been stored away in the old Mitchel Field," which means a search for the files would certainly be an unenviable task. Mitchel Field, which had served as a military base in the early part of the century, is still a big place geographically. It was part of the projected and now defunct Staten Island Homeport, and houses Navy personnel, but the Nassau County government also leases parts of the property for some of its own agencies, including the District Attorney's Office, the County Police Department, and state-supported Nassau Community College.

Digging for the records relating to Caputo's past, in preparation for a trial, is only part of the problem facing prosecutors in Nassau County. There's also his present to contend with—his present state of mind and his attorney's present inclinations and stratagems.

Following his surrender, there were a series of

court appearances scheduled in quick succession. On March 16, 1994, the day before the broadcast of Caputo's "Prime Time" national confession, attorney Michael Kennedy pressed for his client's initial psychiatric evaluation *outside* the confines of the Nassau County Correctional Center. Scrupulous in court and ever polite, Kennedy stayed on the offensive on behalf of his client.

"As you know," he began steadily, "I said last week this man belongs in a psychiatric hospital and needs psychiatric care and he needs medication. And Your Honor, very kindly and to the extent the court could do anything, said that you did want him to receive the appropriate psychiatric treatment, and that medication seemed appropriate.

"Judge, he's gotten none of that. He's been languishing in a facility here in Nassau County where he has not been treated well. I'm not saying any more than that. He's certainly not being treated the way a man who is incarcerated under a 7.30 commitment order for mental incompetency should be treated."

Kennedy didn't get his way. The judge ordered that a state-appointed psychiatrist from the Department of Mental Hygiene immediately examine Caputo at the Nassau County jail. Within two days everyone was back in court.

Judge Dunne, taking his seat behind the bench, kept his remarks brief.

"All right, ladies and gentlemen, counselors. I guess you are aware that the report by the psychiatrist was received this morning. We have made copies, I believe, for the applicable parties. In conclusion, and I'll only read one line, 'Mr. Caputo is fit to proceed with trial.' "

Kennedy was given time to determine whether he wanted another psychiatric examination performed. Judge Dunne set the matter down for a next appearance on March 30, but not before addressing a final issue, the press coverage, hardly an inappropriate concern given the level of press attention the case was again receiving, much of it generated by Michael Kennedy.

"Counselors," the judge said in a voice that was on the stern side of serious, "before you leave, I would just want to make mention of the Disciplinary Rules, particularly those under DR 717 regarding trial publicity. You have just received documents, for example, which may be protected for the benefit of the defendant and may not. I'm not sure, nor am I stating that DR 717 is applicable at this point. But before we proceed to attempt to try this case in the public court rather than in the court as set down by law, I want everyone to review the Disciplinary Rules. And to act accordingly."

Kennedy wasn't going to take it personally, but he fashioned a shrewd response. "I think that's appropriate, Judge. I can tell you it's the defense's position that the documents provided to us this morning are in fact confidential to these particular proceedings, and are not to be handed out to the press. And they will not be."

Veteran Assistant District Attorney George Peck was assigned to handle the initial proceedings. He stepped in during those first weeks but would soon have to leave to take over another huge case looming on the horizon: the trial of Colin Ferguson, the accused Long Island Railroad gunman. Peck had his hands full getting ready to tangle with the formidable civil rights attorney William Kunstler. The renowned court fighter was preparing a so-called "black rage" defense on Ferguson's behalf, based on the novel but not unprecedented notion that certain violent acts can be explained and perhaps defended as justifiable because the perpetrator had been rendered incapable of sound judgment by years of oppression and psychological disfigurement. Kunstler was going to soon command all of Peck's attention, so the Caputo case was steered to another old pro, Dan Cotter.

Cotter had earned his stripes through years of handling sensitive cases in which any mishandling by the prosecutor's office might have set off embarrassing public and political recriminations and unrelenting assaults by the ever-sensitive press corps. One such case was the prosecution of Robert Golub, who Cotter was able to convict of the crime of murdering Kelly Ann Tinyes, the teenage next-door neighbor whose mutilated body was found cramped in a crawl space in her own home.

On March 30, then, it was the avuncular, bearlike

Cotter going against his flip side, the intense and meticulous Michael Kennedy, before Judge Dunne.

Kennedy's opener: his client, the confessed serial killer Ricardo S. Caputo, was ready to stand trial.

"I do not intend to contest the findings of his ability to participate in these proceedings and to understand them," Kennedy intoned. "I will file my formal intention to proffer psychiatric testimony and evidence in this particular case."

Cotter rose and responded in his low-key but assertive style, anxious to show that his office was set to go.

"I move at this time to confirm the report of the Kirby Forensic Psychiatric Center, specifically that it is Dr. Kirschner's report that the defendant at this time is fit to proceed to trial. That's number one . . ."

He paused.

"Number two, I've had conversations with counsel and I indicated that while he is in the process of serving me with formal notice, I will prepare subpoenas and try to get whatever documents from whatever institutions are appropriate to facilitate examinations by his psychiatrist, in addition to the People's psychiatrist. Basically the People are ready to proceed to trial at this time with the exception now of the psychiatric notice."

Tit for tat, no one was giving in. The proceedings were put off for another month.

* * *

It would be a bad month for the members of the prosecution team. First they learned the original grand jury minutes from the 1971 case could not be located. In fact, they were believed to have been destroyed in a building fire at Mitchel Field several years earlier. Prosecutors now faced the prospect of bringing the case in to a new grand jury from ground zero—a case more than two decades old! And Cotter was off the case, having been appointed as a district court judge.

The case was handed off again, this time to an aggressive assistant named Elise McCarthy, one of the recent additions to the elite Major Offense Bureau. Poring into the case in a race to catch up, McCarthy started with a run of good fortune: it was as if the case of Natalie Brown's murder had been preserved in a time warp—all the witnesses and detectives who were initially involved were reachable! She found them, reorganized the evidence, took it all before the secret grand jury panel, and on May 11 a new indictment was handed up against Ricardo Caputo. This time, though, there were two counts: not only was he reindicted on the initial charge of intentional murder, he was also now being charged with murder under the theory that he acted under circumstances evincing a depraved indifference to human life.

Arraignment on the new charges was scheduled for May 16. Caputo was there but stunned everyone, in light of his earlier dramatic televised confession, by remaining mute when Judge Dunne asked him to respond to the charges and enter a plea.

Attorney Simone Monasebian, standing in for lead defense attorney Michael Kennedy, rose quickly to speak on her client's behalf. She said she would enter a not guilty plea for her client because he was unable to understand the charges. "I don't think," she reiterated, "he is capable of giving an informed plea at this time."

Assistant District Attorney Fred Klein, himself standing in for lead prosecutor McCarthy, objected loudly, almost incredulously. Klein was hardly unfamiliar with the legal maneuverings that often attend high-publicity cases—only a year ago he handled one of the country's biggest ever, the infamous soap opera saga of Joey Buttafuoco and Amy Fisher, the teen girlfriend who'd pumped a bullet into the head of Joey's wife.

Klein knew Caputo had recently been found competent to stand trial, knew Michael Kennedy had stipulated to that finding. But Monasebian stood firm on behalf of her silent client: neither she nor Ricardo Caputo were going to be able to say more until *all* the psychiatric evaluations were complete.

It was almost an eerie replay of events twenty-three years ago, after Caputo was arrested and held in jail for Natalie Brown's murder. At that time he was lucid enough to explain to police, in a six-page confession, why he killed his girlfriend. Investigators say there was nothing in that admission about any mental or emotional problems. It was only during his tenure in prison that Caputo raised the question of competency when he allegedly started talking to his victim. His condition prompted the postponement of the trial—until now. And while no one can be sure, perhaps Caputo's silence this time around is a ploy—to postpone the inevitable, or give more credence to the notion that he is mentally unstable.

Determining competency to stand trial is a preliminary but important function in the criminal justice process, but as one expert says, "It's a fluid concept, because the guy who's competent yesterday could conceivably not be next week. It's clear that prior to going to trial, competency will be re-examined any number of times."

Dr. Naftali G. Berrill is a forensic psychologist and faculty member of the John Jay College for Criminal Justice in New York City. He directs the New York Forensic Mental Health Group in New York, and has been called upon in a number of cases to make a diagnosis at the early stages of a trial.

He says, "In order to find a defendant competent, the doctor has to perform tests to determine if he or she can understand the charges, cooperate with an attorney, and demonstrate an understanding of the judicial system." But Dr. Berrill makes clear an important distinction that sometimes gets lost in a layman's understanding of the process. "You can be mentally ill and competent. In fact, you can be quite crazy and still demonstrate an adequate understanding of the things you need to know, and therefore be found fit to proceed at trial."

Dr. Berrill had the opportunity to determine competency in two recent Long Island cases in which the defendants were accused of, or admitted to, killing many people. Berrill examined Long Island Railroad gunman Colin Ferguson and found him fit to stand trial. Dr. Berrill says Ferguson fits the profile of "mass murderer," one who commits explosive acts out of rage, depression, or paranoia, and who may even gloat over the attention his actions receive. Ferguson commanded attention during his initial court appearances, asserting himself through statements and pointed questions to the judge. Dr. Berrill says he even saw the defendant being interviewed on television, a move he questioned.

"Here is this fellow who fails to achieve, to accomplish, and I think he is ultimately hurting himself by doing this. He may not have the insight or wherewithal to see that, but is just pleased to be in this dialogue with someone on television. I don't know what he accomplishes. But in my way of thinking, if there is any doubt about his competency to go forward, this negates that and it would convince anyone watching the interview that this was not a madman. He was lucid and clear."

Admitted serial killer Joel Rifkin stood trial and was ultimately convicted of murder in Nassau County. The jury found him criminally responsible for his actions. After his capture, he told authorities that he killed and mutilated seventeen women, many of them prostitutes. Dr. Berrill conducted an interview of the suspect during preliminary proceedings. "I felt he wasn't competent to waive his Miranda warning. I felt he had been up for four or five days on end and he was decompensating. And apart from what his reason was for killing these people, I think he was deteriorated in his thinking and reasoning. As a consequence, he made some stupid decisions which ultimately got him caught. And instead of asking for an attorney, he, in classic—almost manic—fashion, just shared with the police all the killings he'd done. There's no reason to do that. With an attorney present, he probably wouldn't have done that."

Smart lawyers, then, are sure to keep their client's mouth shut. Or carefully craft their statements—even actions and appearances—in such a way that's helpful to their defense. Then they hire the best expert their client's money can buy to bolster their argument in testimony during a trial.

Attorney Michael Kennedy has already lined up the expert who would perform that final evaluation of Ricardo Caputo, an expert who was the favorite of prosecutors nationwide, who'd testified for the government in the explosive trials of Jeffrey Dahmer in Wisconsin and Arthur Shawcross of upstate New York. In fact, Dr. Park Dietz was at that very moment in a courtroom down the hall from Judge Dunne's chambers, testifying for Nassau County in the case against Joel Rifkin.

Dr. Park Dietz, popular and sought-after by prosecutors all over the map, was a straightforward nononsense witness whose explanations cut impressively through the usual medical mumbo-jumbo and made the complicated terminology easy for a jury to understand. He might have been the perfect expert witness, the one to wrap it up quickly, in the case against Ricardo Caputo.

But in the inevitable battle between dueling expert witnesses, the tables in Judge Dunne's courtroom had dramatically turned. Dietz might have been the best man—but Michael Kennedy had gotten to him first.

CHAPTER TWENTY

Prisoner #94002367 has a routine no different from that of any other prisoner in the maximum security wing of the Nassau County Correctional Center in East Meadow, Long Island. Except that, at present, Ricardo Caputo gets a little extra attention.

He was admitted to the prison on March 10, 1994, the day after his return to New York from Argentina and his bombshell confession on national television. Because he's considered an escape risk, he's been spending his time in one of twenty cells on the floor of "A" tier, an observation tier. A correction officer is assigned around the clock to stand outside the cells in that tier; but prison spokesman Lieutenant Bob Anderson says that except for that distinction, Caputo is simply part of the general population and has the same privileges as everyone else.

There are indoor and outdoor recreation centers and an interior gym where inmates can play anything from basketball to ping-pong. Caputo could even play checkers if he wanted to, the game he said he enjoyed playing with the brothers of Natalie Brown, his first murder victim.

Caputo is escorted to and from his cell, a stark and simple space. A bed is affixed to one wall, and adjacent to the bed, a commode and sink with an unbreakable mirror. There are two shelves with hooks below. Caputo's wardrobe is prison issue, orange shirts and pants. He has the option of wearing his own clothes for court appearances.

His everyday routine starts at five-thirty A.M. The lights-out time is ten P.M. In between there are three standard meals a day: bacon and eggs, or cereal, juice and fruit for breakfast; a sandwich or spaghetti for lunch; and hot meals for dinner that are wheeled into the tiers on food carts.

If the place looks different to Caputo now than it did twenty-three years ago, it's because the prison has undergone a massive overhaul in recent years. Even the cement-block walls in the visiting area have been spruced up, and are now painted in bright orange, yellow, and blue. The glaring fluorescent lights leave little room for privacy. Caputo, if he has visitors, may speak to them across a partitionless barrier between the hours of noon and four P.M. and then four P.M. to eight weeknights.

Since his return to the prison, guards report no trouble with their notorious charge—a difference already from his stay in 1971, when, within weeks of leading police to the Flower Hill home where he'd left the stabbed and lifeless body of victim Natalie Brown, he began talking to the deceased. Those mindless verbal meanderings were the basis for the finding that he was incompetent to aid in his own defense or to stand trial.

The memory of those "conversations" with the dead Natalie Brown are no doubt on the mind of defense attorney Michael Kennedy, who has notified the court that he plans to pursue an insanity defense. Through his well-planned media blitz, he's already spread the word that Caputo suffers from a condition the lawyer calls "multiple personality disorder." In his so-called diaries, compiled in Argentina before his return to New York, Caputo himself had written of his three distinct personas.

Kennedy is no stranger to risks, or to the "Lights! Cameras! Action!" aspect of attention-getting cases. His history at the bar reveals a man more than willing to take on almost insurmountable challenges in an attempt to beat the odds. In the mature years of his career, his aristocratic bearing perhaps obscures his radical beginnings when, as a young trial lawyer in San Francisco, he represented clients ranging from LSD guru Timothy Leary and the militant anti–Vietnam War activists known collectively as the "Chicago 8." When he moved to New York, he took on cases on behalf of members of the Irish Republican Army. He later defended one of the key figures in the massive organized crime "Pizza Connection" case. Kennedy also appealed the conviction of Jean Harris, the convicted killer of Scarsdale Diet doctor Herman Tarnower.

But Michael Kennedy always ran a diversified

practice, as demonstrated by his decision to take on Ivana Trump's divorce case against her mega-developer husband Donald Trump.

Ricardo Caputo is Michael Kennedy's latest challenge, especially given Kennedy's early decision to commit to an insanity defense that will focus on "multiple personality disorder."

Some experts say this psychiatric diagnosis has become so popular recently, it's almost the defense du jour in insanity cases. But a hurdle for Kennedy and his client is that in New York few documented cases of this nature exist; members of the legal and psychiatric professions are sure to be watching this one closely.

Kennedy had told the *New York Times* at one point that he would have preferred to avoid a trial by entering a plea of "not criminally responsible," which would have meant, according to the news report, that Caputo would be sent to a psychiatric hospital. But such a plea would have to be agreed to by both sides, and Nassau County Prosecutor Elise McCarthy has suggested she has no interest for now in signing off on that plea.

So instead, the pretrial skirmishes that will set the tone for the trial of Ricardo Caputo are focusing on the task of shoring up expert witnesses and arranging for those experts to interview the confessed killer.

While Kennedy is undoubtedly plotting his strategy very carefully for the upcoming trial in Nassau County, it's possible *all* the murder cases against

Ricardo Caputo in the United States might be consolidated, necessitating a single winner-take-all courtroom war.

Noted New York attorney Benjamin Brafman doubts that, saying, "I don't think one jurisdiction is necessarily going to be bound by the jury finding in another jurisdiction, because the standards in those states could be different, the timing could be different. You know, you could be crazy on Monday and not be crazy on Tuesday."

To bolster his insanity defense, Kennedy will also fight to suppress the six-page confession to Natalie Brown's murder that Caputo dictated in the hours after his arrest in 1971. Detectives and prosecutors who took the statement say to this day that Caputo was lucid, and that there was never any mention of "voices," or of any other emotional disturbances.

But "multiple personality disorder" diagnoses have been used in many cases outside New York, one of the most notable being that of the "Hillside Strangler" in Los Angeles. At that time, in the mid-eighties, experts were sharply divided over whether suspect Kenneth Bianchi truly suffered from the syndrome.

Dr. Robert Berger, Director of Forensic Psychiatry at Bellevue Hospital Center in New York, is not surprised at the stubborn lack of consensus on the syndrome. The multiple personality argument, he says, comes with built-in complications and contradictions.

"The first problem is with the diagnosis itself," Dr. Berger asserts. "There's a degree of controversy as to whether the diagnosis exists, and also *when* it exists. Camps have developed within the field of psychiatry that are divided between those who believe and those who simply don't." Dr. Berger says the result of the internecine debate is that "those who don't believe have a tendency to underdiagnose or not diagnose the condition too frequently, while those who believe in it tend to diagnose too frequently, and too quickly. The reality probably lies somewhere in between."

Berger also says the courts are hardly uniform in how they deal with the disorder when it's raised as an issue by the defense.

"Experts who are firm believers in the illness say the courts are looking at 'multiple personality' in the wrong context. In an attempt to look at things in a concrete way, some courts say, 'Let's try one particular personality, in reality we're talking about a person, not different personalities, but all of these multiples in one person. You have to try the individual.' "

Another noted attorney experienced in the use of the insanity defense calls it "the hardest defense in the world." Marvyn Kornberg represented former mental patient Steven Smith in a Manhattan murder case, but the jury didn't buy the insanity defense and found Smith guilty of killing Bellevue Hospital doctor Kathryn Hinnant. Smith was a homeless man who wandered the underbelly of the massive hospital complex before confronting his victim in her office. He claimed he heard voices that ordered him to kill.

Kornberg says the most important thing is to persuade the jury to get past its initial negative perception of the case—and of the defendant.

"With an insanity defense," Kornberg reiterates, "you are already admitting that your client committed the crime." If it's a particularly horrendous crime, you're in trouble. "The jurors are already looking at you with a jaundiced eye, as if you have horns sticking out of your head."

But attorney Brafman, considering the chain of events since Caputo surrendered, says the carefully crafted confession might go a long way in selling an insanity defense.

"Assume," Brafman muses, "that the facts are that for the past twenty years he's lived a productive life, a normal life, and he decides, 'Look, I'm tired of living this secret life. I was crazy when I did those things. I go back, I have a good lawyer work out this defense, I have my team of experts lined up in advance to agree that this is a workable defense.'" Brafman hits on another point. "These cases are twenty years old, forensically, they're not going to be easy to prosecute. Who knows if the witnesses are around? So maybe you can pull this off and convince a jury you were insane at the time, and you're found not guilty. And then you're able to convince a panel of experts that you're no longer insane!"

Brafman takes a beat.

"Then, they'd have no right to hold you . . ."

But that's speculation for now. If Ricardo Caputo is found not guilty by reason of insanity, he will be sent away to a state-run mental institution. If he is convicted of second degree murder in the Natalie Brown case, he faces the maximum sentence of life in prison.

There's one possibility that could reduce the ultimate length of incarceration for Caputo if he is sentenced to prison: a jury could consider the lesser charge of manslaughter in the first degree. That finding would depend on a belief that "the person acted under the influence of extreme emotional disturbance for which there was a reasonable explanation or excuse, the reasonableness of which is to be determined from the viewpoint of a person in the defendant's situation under circumstances as the defendant believed them to be." Manslaughter carries a minimum prison term of two to six years and a maximum $8\frac{1}{3}$ to twenty-five years behind bars. It would be a tough sell, but if anyone would pitch it with a fair chance of success, it would be an attorney like Michael Kennedy.

While everyone awaits the spectacle of a trial of the multiple killer who murdered women he truly loved, the medical profession continues to take steps to clarify the multiple personality issue. Dr. Berger says the *Diagnostic Statistical Manual of Mental Disorders,* the so-called bible of the profession put out by the American

Psychiatric Association, has for the first time sought to standardize the criteria for this particular diagnosis.

"There's an interview scale that's been put together," Berger explains. "It poses certain kinds of questions, and should you get certain responses— and a certain number of them—then they suggest that the likelihood of the disorder being present is higher or lower, depending on that individual's score."

The lawyers agree, however, that if the case goes to trial as quickly as it's likely to, both sides will be lining up their respective psychiatric experts. Lawyer Kornberg says, somewhat cynically, "It becomes a dollars and cents battle. Who can present the biggest name or the psychiatrist with the fanciest credentials. It boils down to this, especially for the defendant: How much money can you spend on credentials?"

It also matters, Kornberg says, that the expert with the credentials can and will be willing to play to the jury. "You have to present a psychiatrist who can sell himself to the jury, it's true; but you also have to get a jury that's intelligent enough to understand that they're not simply freeing a man when they judge him to be not guilty by reason of insanity. The jurors must be helped to understand that you can commit crimes—real crimes—because of psychiatric problems." It can be a problem of semantics too, for jurors. "Part of the problem is that the verdict is 'Not guilty by reason of insanity,' and to use the words 'not guilty' when someone has already admitted the commission of a crime is a difficult concept for many jurors to understand."

"It would be easier," Kornberg concludes, "if the verdict was 'guilty' by reason of insanity. Too often, especially if you think your guy *is* nuts, the jurors think if they say the words 'Not guilty,' they'd be acquitting your man and just walking him out."

But Brafman, a lawyer who always considers the political implications of results in the courtroom, says the sheer notoriety of this case makes it prohibitively unlikely that Caputo will experience any version of freedom anytime soon, even if he ends up being delivered back into the mental health system.

"The likelihood of someone being willing to take the responsibility of ordering his release is remote to nonexistent," Brafman says. "Compare this case to that of a guy like Charles Manson." He let the comparison sink in. "Nobody is ever gonna release Ricardo Caputo."

Kennedy will bring his experts and his unparalleled ability to persuade, just the same. A profile of the lawyer in *New York* magazine hinted at just how aware he is of the latter ability. While Kennedy refused to be interviewed for the article—he's extremely selective about his choices of interviewers and interview subjects—he did allow *New York* to review notes he'd prepared for the actor Raul Julia, who was studying at the time for his lead role in the movie of Scott Turow's book, *Presumed Innocent*."

The words Michael Kennedy put in the actor's mouth were ideas, not lines of dialogue, presumably tailored to coach the actor in the specific role.

"In truth, we [lawyers] do care a lot about the performance. Certainly more than we care about the production, or the truth. We need to do well even if the production fails or the truth is lost. Tactical considerations supplant ethical ones . . ." Kennedy's notes continued.

Ricardo Caputo's hopes for liberty were in the hands of a lawyer so confident, he had his client admit to the worst things anyone dare admit about oneself.

CHAPTER TWENTY-ONE

Throughout his life, Ricardo Caputo eluded authorities—and his horrible past—by slipping through the cracks of a day-to-day existence. Based on his own account, he learned at a youthful age the labors of survival, and the skills served him well as he went from job to job, city to city, relationship to relationship, and ultimately, murder to murder. As a result, these learned behaviors became second nature to Caputo, allowing him to adapt with ease to new surroundings and identities. Caputo may have also viewed as a mark of success his ability to hone these skills in such a cunning and clever enough fashion as to elude law enforcement officials for more than two decades. So it comes as no surprise when, after talking to the experts, Ricardo Caputo invites debate and defies standard definition when attempts are made to categorize him for a traditional psychological profile.

Caputo earned the dubious distinction of "serial killer" when news accounts splashed the details of his surrender on their front pages. *New York Newsday*'s headline screamed, ODYSSEY OF DEATH. SERIAL SLAYER: 'I WANT TO FACE THE PAST.' The *New York Times* wrote,

DRIFTER'S TALE OF SERIAL DEATH: REMORSE PROMPTS CONFESSION. But does Ricardo Caputo's actions fit the profile of a *serial* killer? Does one think of him in the same category as Joel Rifkin, who admitted to killing seventeen women in and around the New York metropolitan area? Or the recently executed John Wayne Gacy, who was convicted of killing thirty-three young men, many of whose bodies were discovered underneath the crawl space of his Illinois home? Or Jeffrey Dahmer, the Milwaukee man whose apartment held the body parts and skeletal remains of eleven victims?

The sheer numbers suggest otherwise; Caputo admits to four murders and authorities link him to a fifth. The statistics don't reach into double digits; nevertheless they are undoubtedly a clear representation of a killer who repeated his behavior again and again. But the number of victims alone doesn't define the serial killer; rather, it's the pattern of behavior and the reasons behind it that is investigated and examined.

Dr. Naftali G. Berrill even questions whether there is a "classic serial type."

"If there is a classic profile," he says, "this person is generally an antisocial personality, but not in the sense that he's necessarily a gun-toting, bank-robbing type guy. These personalities are characteristically quiet in demeanor, not noticed. Usually, at their core is a very intense anger, and simultaneous with this anger a kind of sexual perverse fixation. Sex and violence go hand in hand with serial killers. Usually they'll have sex with their victims before, during, and after the killings. They're sexual sadists. And the other common thread that runs through as part of their antisocial behavior—other than the fact that they are committing these heinous crimes—is that there's an obvious failure to feel anything for the victim; there's a lack of empathy."

Dr. Berrill has firsthand experience in dealing with an admitted killer who by all public accounts seems to fit the "classic" description to a tee. Berrill interviewed Joel Rifkin during pretrial hearings to determine the defendant's competency to stand trial. While the doctor thought Rifkin was in a deteriorated mental state at the time of his arrest, Rifkin nevertheless was brought to trial as his attorney argued an insanity defense. The Long Island man was subsequently convicted and found criminally responsible for his actions. Without referring to Rifkin specifically, Dr. Berrill described a serial killer profile that mirrors Rifkin's case.

"The killer chooses his victims because they are easy targets, they are generally people who won't hurt him." The doctor says in case studies, three groups of people surface again and again: children, young women, and homosexuals. "These are segments of the population that can be considered vulnerable," he says. The doctor also includes prostitutes in this group, because, he claims, they are constantly taking a risk in dealing with people they don't know. When Rifkin was arrested, he told police that he made a habit of cruising known areas of prostitution. Many of his victims, he said, worked the streets.

But Dr. Berrill goes on to say that prostitutes aren't necessarily pinpointed in any literal sense. "It doesn't mean that a prostitute hurt the killer when he was little. It could be a replaying of some aspect of childhood and it might be something symbolic. Perhaps the desire for this sort of conquest derives from feelings of inferiority, feelings of being sexually or personally inadequate. As a consequence, the killer connects to someone who is beneath his contempt. That 'right' situation permits an inordinate amount of rage to be vented."

While on some level—however twisted—the killer "connects" with his victims, there's another level in which there is a purposeful detachment from the targets of a murderer's rage.

"When they commit these kinds of killings," says Dr. Berrill, "there exists a grandiosity, almost a contempt—as opposed to empathy. The killer will sometimes revel in his behavior.

"They don't see their victims as people. If they say they do, they're lying. When the killings occur, the victims cease to be people in the murderer's mind. They're prey. The way the hunter goes out for deer, that's exactly the quality the victims take on for the perpetrators."

Whether Ricardo Caputo fits the mold is something a jury may have to ultimately decide. Prosecutors will no doubt try to convince the jury that Caputo knew what he was doing and what he was about to do as he courted, then murdered, his victims. They may portray him as the most vicious of predators whose sole objective was to find young, attractive, successful women whom he could ultimately seduce and then destroy in a lethal, vengeful fit of rage. In fact, one of the two murder counts lodged against him accuses Caputo of committing *intentional* murder. But by Caputo's own account, there was never a hint of premeditation. He describes relationships in which he says he was in love, or looking for love. There were dating, or live-in situations—nothing in his mind that could be characterized as a casual affair. Caputo felt that at some levels he bonded with these women, and it appears as if he wanted to do so in a serious and lasting way. Was he trying to fill his need for love and affection—the basics he claims he never had as a child? Did he kill because he realized, when these women rejected him, that his needs would never be met? Or was he cunningly ambitious, and in his attempts to climb the proverbial social ladder, latched on to women of means—only to learn that he was in over his head with unrealistic expectations and a perverted sense of himself? Did self-hate spawn the stranglings and stompings of a madman?

Perhaps future analysis will answer those questions. For now, Caputo claims that the victims demanded too much of him, that he couldn't fulfill their needs.

He said the conflict and confusion prompted voices in his head, voices that planted him squarely and motivated him along his lethal path.

If that's the case, Dr. Berrill says, then there's the possible diagnosis of an "atypical schizophrenic." The doctor characterizes the illness as one including severe delusions, grandiose feelings and thoughts, with "command" hallucinations that, even though rare, are identified by the notion that orders are given or heard compelling someone to do something.

"This killer is different from someone who is sort of cunning and predatory and sociopathic and sadistic," the doctor says. "They may effect a murder by virtue of the fact that they are quite delusional when they are doing the killing. They can't separate or understand the wrongfulness of their act."

Caputo might, in fact, agree with that assessment. He claims he didn't know what he was doing when he killed these women. "Only a crazy guy would do that," he told ABC's Chris Wallace. But Dr. Ira Kramer endorses the alternate explanation offered by Dr. Berrill. Kramer is a clinical psychologist, and Director for the New York Center for Addiction Treatment Services. He doesn't believe Caputo is a "serial killer" in the classic sense of the term.

"He's not a 'psychopath' in the way people use the term. Actually, it's a 'pop' term, not even a technical one, and it's used to define a madman who's crazy all the time, who lives an isolated life, who goes around killing people and thinks about it all the time."

The doctor believes the case of Ricardo Caputo is something different, and he underscores his analysis by using the Tony Curtis movie, *The Great Impostor*, and Woody Allen's movie, *Zelig*, as examples. In those movies, the title characters take on different personas, even different professions, and excel in them to the highest degree.

"These guys were sociopaths," according to Dr. Kramer. "When they were in their role, doing their thing, they really weren't fooling anybody. They were good. It wasn't an act. Their behavior was real."

Dr. Kramer believes Ricardo Caputo could be considered a sociopath. According to his definition, "A sociopath is better than the average person when he's in a positive state. He's smarter, more devoted, loyal, sensitive—all these great things. And we can live with the good things. The problems begin when the sociopath swings in the negative direction."

According to Dr. Kramer, both the good and bad behaviors are equally extreme, and while a sociopath can be truly engaging or talented while on his best behavior, he can be the most horrible of monsters at his worst. Dr. Kramer says it's quite possible that Caputo may have actually been one of the best and most talented waiters in a popular Chicago restaurant where he tallied up record sales and had customers asking for him long after he was gone.

"Everybody loved him? So that's a sociopath—he's better than good."

And the doctor doesn't disagree with the notion

that Caputo is gifted on many levels. Time and time again, with girlfriend after girlfriend, Caputo demonstrated his artistic talent, his flair for languages, and his athletic abilities.

"When they're in a positive state," the doctor asserts, "they're really extraordinary. And it's not that they're fooling anybody; they're truly gifted."

Dr. Kramer says when Caputo returned to his homeland and disclosed the horrible events of his life to Argentinean psychiatrist Dr. Fernando Linares, it was reasonable for Linares to make a preliminary diagnosis of schizophrenia. But Dr. Kramer believes Caputo's violent actions can be attributed to what he calls a "schizophrenic episode." And he says it may be that his South American colleague may have been trying to explain away something similar based on the information that came forward after his initial examinations of Caputo. Dr. Kramer suggests that Caputo was in a "dissociative state" when he committed the vicious acts.

"He really doesn't have two personalities. People who suffer from multiple personalities really *have* multiple personalities. Caputo—he was the waiter. He was one guy his whole life. But there was a state in which he would find himself which would be completely separate. That state is a violent state. It's not a separate personality. He's still one person. It's just that there is some kind of trigger that brings this about."

Dr. Kramer has seen hundreds of patients in similar circumstances. He says in many cases the "trigger" for the violent or destructive behavior stems from at least one or as many as a combination of three chemical and/or physiological factors: drugs and alcohol, acute schizophrenia, or manic depression. The doctor raises the question as to whether Caputo was a substance abuser. Caputo himself makes no mention of this kind of problem, although the news accounts of the brutal murder of Laura Maria Gomez Saenz in Mexico City in 1977 reveal that empty liquor bottles had been strewn all over the ravaged apartment.

Dr. Kramer also hesitates to characterize Caputo as a full-blown schizophrenic. The doctor says the illness can be diagnosed if a patient is actively hallucinating. But is there a measure of how often Caputo suffered from hallucinations and to what degree they disrupted his life? He claims there were episodes when he heard voices or when he didn't feel he was himself. But Dr. Kramer says a patient is not technically schizophrenic, even calls it "a little unusual," when there are periods of hallucinations that last temporarily and don't resurface for several years.

If Dr. Kramer isn't convinced that Ricardo Caputo is schizophrenic, Dr. Berrill isn't so sure of the claim of multiple personality disorder. Berrill says controversy swirls around the issue; in fact, professionals don't all agree with the diagnosis—what the so-called illness means and how it comes about. The doctor says the *Diagnostic Manual*—the experts' so-called bible—has even moved away from the term. Dr. Berrill says he's only met one patient that he truly believed suffered from the disorder. In that case, the patient had been the victim of sexual and emotional abuse from members of the immediate family.

Caputo, however, makes the same claim, saying he was abandoned and sexually victimized in his youth. But again, experts disagree on what role that plays in future, severe mental disorders, and they say that more often than not there are other factors involved in the mix. If and whether it contributes to a multiple personality, Dr. Berrill says, multiple personality disorder may be very hard to prove in a court of law. But it's a challenge that attorney Michael Kennedy is not afraid to take on in the legal arena, where perhaps he may break new ground arguing the reputed illness as part of an insanity defense. He won't speculate, but Dr. Berrill—long experienced in examining controversial defendants and testifying in these cases —provides a sobering thought on what the outcome of the case might be.

"Of all the serial killers that went to trial, I don't know of one that was found not guilty by reason of insanity."

When asked if he was talking historically, or if he was referring to trials in recent memory, the doctor responded, "In *any* memory. I don't know of any."

CHAPTER TWENTY-TWO

The media has played a key role in the life and times of Ricardo Caputo, from the initial news reports of the gruesome stabbing death of Natalie Brown to his portrayal as a hunted serial killer on shows like "America's Most Wanted."

But in what's been described as a brilliantly orchestrated campaign, defense attorney Michael Kennedy managed to turn Caputo's admission of unspeakable inhumanity into a successful ploy for considerable public sympathy. In essence, Caputo was claiming to be a "victim" of the "voices" he says he heard, and after he stopped hearing them, had lived something close to a model life as husband and father. Reporters searched for clues to support the story of the killer's subsequent "model life" and found some, but were hard-pressed for an explanation about the "remorse" and "sorrow" he says he came to feel so acutely when it wasn't voices but rather the screams of his victims that he began to hear.

It's part of an increasing trend in which lawyers have become adept at using the media as an effective tool in the arsenal of their defense. It's a tool that can control the flow of information, on the one hand, and on the other, counter the prosecution's traditional stranglehold on offensive tactical strikes.

Attorney Ronald Kuby, who has recently shared the defense table with famed lawyer William Kunstler in the cases of the Long Island Railroad gunman Colin Ferguson and the Islamic Fundamentalist bombers of the World Trade Center in lower Manhattan, says Kennedy seized a significant moment after Caputo's surrender and then "just ran with it."

"He recognized," Kuby said, "that being first and jumping in with his client's own controlled account of what happened gave him a tremendous opportunity, one which criminal defense lawyers ordinarily never get. We're usually 'reactives.' The State almost always moves first against our clients, portraying them as the devils or demons or the worst thing to hit the planet since the last thing that was the worst thing to hit the planet."

Kennedy's colleagues believe almost unanimously that it's unlikely he will ever have his client testify during the trial—all the more reason, other lawyers say, that it was so important that he got Caputo to tell *his* version of the story in a public forum.

"Kennedy has allowed Caputo's story to be told in the first person," says Lawyer Ben Brafman, "without his client ever having to be cross-examined. That's really a coup. You put somebody on the stand and let an aggressive, talented prosecutor cross-examine him, and I don't care how truthful or well-prepared the client is, his story is never going to come out a hundred percent in his favor."

Kennedy's opening move then, was a pre-emptive attempt to neutralize what most attorneys argue is the pro-prosecution atmosphere that usually surrounds and greatly influences the press coverage of a case. Part of it is that the press is like the public—in fact, by definition, they *are* the public's eyes and ears. And the vast majority of the public tends to think that if someone's indicted and is being taken to trial, then he's guilty and will only escape the net if some clever lawyer finds a loophole.

But beyond public perception, there's the reality that's become tradition of how the machinery of the criminal justice system works. Following the arrest of a wanted suspect, there's usually the initial flurry of law enforcement news conferences and the subsequent "leak, don't speak" strategy that limits reporters' access to contravening facts or probabilities. Lawyers on the defense bar are fond of saying the government agencies, with their sometimes vast public relations departments and layers of spin control, always play with a stacked deck.

Lawyer Brafman says the successful defense lawyer has to find ways to counter that.

"When you're on the defense side of a criminal case," he explains, "rarely is the initial burst of publicity about that case positive. In orchestrating *this* case, Kennedy has, for some, turned the story of an admitted serial killer into an almost 'David Jantzen as

The Fugitive' romantic tale. Kennedy did a terrific job in that respect," Brafman says admiringly.

Judges, of course, have become increasingly aware of defense tactics involving media manipulation and have sought to hold the line on anything that could prejudice the case or damage the chances for a fair trial.

In the initial court proceedings following Caputo's surrender, Judge John Dunne reminded the lawyers emphatically about ethics and disciplinary rules and confidentiality restrictions pertaining to the dissemination of protected materials.

And, in that courtroom atmosphere, speaking out of bounds or careening around the rules can win the offending attorney a heap of trouble, as one controversial New York defense lawyer, Bruce Cutler, can attest. Cutler was recently convicted in a nonjury trial of violating the so-called Rule 7 when he spoke to reporters during the 1992 racketeering trial of mob Godfather John Gotti. Rule 7 states simply that an attorney is not supposed to discuss certain details of a pending case in such a way that it might prejudice the trial.

Cutler says that was never his intention.

"I wanted to ensure a level playing field," he said. "And we couldn't, and all I succeeded in doing was getting cited for contempt."

Cutler is appealing his conviction. But while the unprecedented action has sent a chill through the legal community, Michael Ross, an expert in legal ethics, says that in his handling so far of Ricardo Caputo, Michael Kennedy's approach has broken no rules.

"What he did was somewhat novel," Ross observes, "but nothing remarkable. In fact, a recent appellate division decision in upstate New York upheld a lawyer's specific right to hold a news conference in the middle of a murder trial." Ross explained that the news conference was in a small town with only one television station.

Any news conference on the tabloid-fantasy Caputo case called by Michael Kennedy would take place astride the media capital of the world. In New York City, at present, there are more than five thousand people walking around with official New York Police Department press cards, the ultimate credential in terms of unquestioned media access. Four major daily newspapers plus dozens of smaller publications have blanketed the Caputo story, as have two all-news radio stations, every tabloid TV show, plus a handful of prime-time shows based on crime subjects, six major television stations, three all-news cable television outfits, and any number of print and broadcast magazines.

What those numbers mean is that Michael Kennedy's opening gambits will have the effect of familiarizing almost any potential juror with the case, even if it's subliminal. And since he's admitted to murders on both coasts of the United States as well as a neighbor to the south whose relationship to the United

States is sensitive, to say the least, the trial in Nassau County will at once be a national and international story.

Lawyer Ron Kuby says, " 'You want jurors walking in and saying, 'Oh, yeah, I think I remember hearing something about this poor, sick, crazy guy who was so driven by guilt that when he felt better he came in and confessed.' Jurors are not gonna remember details, and it doesn't matter if they do. It's important to set the tone, and Kennedy did it brilliantly."

Brafman adds, "If you have a jury coming in that already knows Caputo's story, the story you helped them to know, then you've done as much as you could on your client's behalf to start a trial and not be at a disadvantage."

And consider the disadvantages the prosecution starts out with. There may be relatively few people in Nassau County who remember in any detail the Natalie Brown murder some twenty-three years ago. Forensically, in this and the other Caputo cases, it may be difficult to put together an unassailable chain of evidence because of the sheer time involved. In Mexico City, for example, officials are already saying they just cannot locate the vital records relating to the beastly murder of Laura Gomez.

Prosecutors in the Caputo cases are facing the psychologically daunting challenge of taking an event from the distant past, fast-forwarding it to the present, and somehow, through some means, making the event as graphic and shocking as it was when it happened. The news conferences and the follow-up stories and the follow-up stories and the horrified reactions of the relatives and friends and neighbors of the victims all took place years ago; dredging it all up again, waving a few newspaper clippings, won't have the effect of a display of genuine and fresh horror a witness on the stand would provide.

All that is currently, and effectively, on the table as Ricardo Caputo's first murder trial approaches, is Ricardo Caputo's version of events. That certainly can't hurt defense attorney Kennedy's chances, lawyer Kuby says.

"He's writing on a largely blank slate in the public consciousness," Kuby observed, "unlike us with the Colin Ferguson case. We are literally writing in the blood of the victims of the Long Island Railroad shooting."

Kennedy is also capitalizing on his client's notoriety, coupled with the astounding fact of his public surrender, in order to mute Ricardo Caputo's reputation as a deadly charmer and reveal him to the jury, first and foremost, as a very sick man.

There are, of course, other ways of "using" the media and other motives for doing so. When Long Island attorney Eric Naiburg allowed his infamous client, the "Long Island Lolita," Amy Fisher, to be interviewed by the tabloid show "Inside Edition," he did so only because he had final approval of the questions and the liberty to supply the answers. The motive for the interview? Amy had been slapped with a

$2 million bail, and selling an interview along with book and movie rights to the salacious story was a novel way to finance bail and allow Naiburg to have his client available and at his disposal to plot their defense.

No bail was set for Ricardo Caputo after he surrendered, and it's unlikely it ever will be. There may be no incentive to raise bail, but there's certainly a story to tell. Caputo's brother Alberto says he's writing a book—his own account of Ricardo's story. It's a story Alberto helped shape, through his public statements after Ricardo's surrender. It's a story Michael Kennedy will hope even one juror will believe.

It is also a story that, more than likely, every detective and law enforcement official who's touched or been touched by one of Caputo's cases will find impossible to stomach.

And it's one that the victims' families—whose lives have been torn to pieces and who view this account as a way of getting Ricardo Caputo off the hook—see as purely and completely obscene.

CHAPTER TWENTY-THREE

Margie Lee Brown is married to Ed Brown, the brother of Ricardo Caputo's first victim. Today she's convinced that Caputo's nagging absence and the failure of the system to bring him to justice killed her in-laws as well.

"I would love to have seen their faces," Margie Lee says of Harold and Julie Brown, "if they'd been alive when this guy surrendered. It would have made their day. It made mine, because all these years I felt like this guy was out there killing other girls. He's admitted to four, but do you know, can you ever know if he's telling the truth? You can't trust him."

Her voice rises as she recalls the bitter pain her husband and his family endured after Natalie's death. Natalie's parents lived in the Flower Hill home where their daughter was brutally murdered until 1985 when Harold retired. The couple lived in Florida for several years, and died within a year of each other. Ed and Margie now live in North Carolina, and distance has not been a factor in their effort to keep abreast of the activities in Caputo's case. They plan to come to New York to testify if it's necessary. Ed Brown wants justice for his sister.

"No one will ever know," he says in a tight, strained voice, "what Natalie was really like." He stops before he can speak again, as his thoughts turn to his sister's murderer. "I think he's still dangerous. Anybody capable of killing like he did, can kill again . . ."

The Browns are part of the terrible legacy Ricardo Caputo left behind. His return from the past did more than create a media sensation. It reopened the once-searing wounds of the families of the young women—all of them full of promise and hope—who had seen a smooth-talking stranger with a sympathetic line come into their lives and extract in a most vicious way what was most precious to them.

By his acts Ricardo Caputo could—for all intents and purposes—become another addition to the list of infamous killers whose names have screamed into the public's consciousness by the very nature of the long list of lives they snuffed out. Consider Jack the Ripper, who killed prostitutes in the London night and became a legend. Or Albert De Salvo, the self-confessed Boston Strangler who said he raped at least two thousand women and was charged with murdering and mutilating at least fourteen and perhaps as many as twenty-one. Then there are Joel Rifkin and Arthur Shawcross, recent serial killers in New York State, who killed seventeen and eleven women, mostly prostitutes, respectively. John Wayne Gacy murdered and dismembered thirty-three young boys. And Ted Bundy, who one investigator compared to Caputo because both were charmers extraordinaire, racked up his share of victims. But these men never knew—or cared to know—their prey; the thrill was the kill. On the other hand, Caputo had relationships with his victims, he bonded with them in what may have been his twisted attempts at love. Or perhaps rather than using a knife, or a gun, his weapon was slow, lethal seduction.

Caputo argues that his troubled personality stabilized when he was in these relationships, and there are no indications of violence or criminal behavior during the nearly ten years he's been married to Susana. But law enforcement officials who chased after Caputo for nearly two decades don't buy into the psychiatry theories. They view his contention as a sophisticated excuse.

San Francisco Police Inspector Earl Sanders never thought twice about Caputo's modus operandi. He saw it clear as a bell in the investigation into Barbara Taylor's murder.

"Barbara was going to be his latest meal ticket," Sanders says, "so he was quite charming and as usual met the family and worked his way in with her friends, and into her life and lifestyle. Usually the women were quite infatuated with him. He was the kind of guy who could walk into a room with twenty women in there, and fifteen would want to take him home with them. He was obviously a ladies' man. He had the gift of gab—what I call the bullshit factor."

Sanders joins his law enforcement counterparts scattered across Ricardo Caputo's killing field when he expresses his sympathy for the victims' families and shares their pain.

And the pain is all too real—again—with Caputo's surrender and tale of woe.

"My life has been crushed, and it's the most horrible thing I've ever gone through," says Barbara Ann Taylor's mother Vera. She said she didn't want to watch the "Prime Time" program because, she said, "I don't want to be upset anymore. They've put the story on television before and it has driven me crazy." Vera Taylor stays at home to care for her husband, who suffers from Alzheimer's disease. She doesn't say Ricardo Caputo's name—and doesn't believe his claims about "voices." "I think he's ruined my life, that's all I have to say."

Jane Becker spoke from Connecticut about the effect of Caputo's surrender on her continuing struggle to deal with her daughter Judy's murder twenty-one years ago.

"We were completely shocked," she said when she heard Caputo had surfaced. "As long as he was still alive, we were happy that he was caught. We had all more or less hoped and thought he was dead by now. But I'm not watching any of the shows because I'm still living it."

Mrs. Becker's daughter Jane took a more cynical approach to Caputo's current story.

"There's nothing to lead us to believe that he has changed in any way. He's always been a manipulative person. For whatever reason, I still believe he's manipulating the situation."

And the possibility that Caputo waged internal battles among warring personalities and that his feelings of remorse and sorrow are genuine?

Retired Nassau County Detective William Coningsby doesn't buy it. He took Caputo's six-page confession when Natalie Brown was murdered twenty-three years ago.

"This is a man who has now taken the 'Son of Sam' argument—that 'the voices made me do it.' This is not a dumb man by any means. He knows his way around."

Coningsby recalled what went through his mind that fateful night.

"When you arrest somebody and then take their confession, you become very intimate with that person in a way. I think he had remorse that he killed Natalie—but it wasn't the remorse that said, 'I shouldn't have done it.' It was more like, 'I'm sorry she's gone.'"

The victims will never come back. The families are left with memories—and now with Ricardo Caputo's present attempt to save his own skin, and to stay out of jail.

"I can't stop thinking of the families," says San

Francisco's Inspector Sanders, the Taylors specifically on his mind. "Maybe this part of the story is like closure for Barbara's family and the others too. It must have been hard on the Taylor family every Easter—when her body was discovered. Now, I think of this past Easter, after he came forward, and the rest of the Easters of their lives. Maybe they'll be better knowing he's getting his comeuppance."

What is Sanders's view of the appropriate "comeuppance" for Ricardo Caputo?

"When you're guilty as hell, you either play crazy or you become the victim yourself. They told me he had multiple personalities. I don't have a problem with that," he said with more than a subtle hint of sarcasm. "The remedy I have for that is—try them all —convict them—put them all in jail. And keep them there."